Stripped Down

Publisher © Chelle Bliss & Eden Butler

July 2019

Editor: Silently Judging Your Grammar

Proofreader: Julie Deaton

Cover Design: Lori Jackson

Paperback Formatting: Allusion Graphics

Stripped Down

CHELLE BLISS
EDEN BUTLER

"Then love is sin, and let me sinful be."
—John Donne

Prologue

Johnny

St. Mary's Catholic School for Young Women
New York, NY - May 2007

I wore my sin like armor. It fit me—all those lies. The sneaky, shitty things I did but pretended I didn't. All the low-down, dirty things I saw fit to manage for my own devices because it needed to be done or because it felt damn good to do it.

Being who I was, living the life I did, in the family I did, sin and the weight of it were the least of my worries. It never bothered me—not the drinking or the gambling. Not the violence or the stealing. Most of that shit happened because it was expected, having a father like mine. He did the work his father had done. He ran the *family*. I would too one day. I'd worry about that weight of all our sin when I was an old man. *If* I got to be an old man.

1

But stepping into my little sister's school for what felt like the hundredth time that semester, I swore that weight got heavier with each step I took. It all came down to her, Samantha Nicola, the source of my greatest sin.

"Johnny?" my cousin Dario called behind me as I walked through the hallway next to the cathedral. There was a crowd of girls, some of them in the show my kid sister, Cara, had organized for their senior program. All of them sporting the matching red collared button-ups and gray plaid skirts just on the too-short side to be acceptable by St. Mary's standards.

I nudged Dario in the ribs when he stared a little too long at May Phan, making him lose his grip on the box in his hand.

"Jailbait," I reminded him.

"Sixteen ain't jailbait when I'm only six months older." Dario shrugged.

"Her father or brothers wouldn't see it that way, asshole." He pulled his attention away from the girl when I slapped him in the back of the head and pushed him through the doorway at the end of the hall.

"Finally!" Cara barked as we entered the room, her frown not lessening when Dario handed over the box.

Jesus, she was a pain in the ass. Graduating or not. Kid sister or not, Cara could be an ungrateful shit.

"Where's the box with the blue robe?" She glared at our cousin as if she thought he had a clue what she meant, then she shifted her attention at me. "Well?"

"*Cazzo*, Cara, how the hell..." I shut my mouth when two nuns came through the door and narrowed their eyes as they spotted us. "Sister Maria, Sister Agnes," I greeted, betting the grin I'd shot their way for the entire month I'd been shuttling Cara around and keeping my eye on her after school hadn't worn out its welcome. By the low blush the younger sisters gave me, I guessed I was still in their good graces. "Forgive my language, but my sister..." I nodded to Cara, who'd dropped the box to the floor and dumped out its contents. "You know how worked up she can get when things don't go her way, *si*?"

The women smiled, hiding their expressions behind their hands when my kid sister cursed under her breath.

"Asshole," she said, tossing a roll of ribbon at my head.

I caught it with one hand, dodging a second roll as she stood. "What?" I asked.

"There was another box. A smaller one. We need it. I put it on top, so I know it was in here." She glared at Dario, who was facing the door, nodding at May when she leaned against the wall, motioning for him to follow her out of the room. "Hey, pay attention." When our cousin stepped toward the door, Cara flicked the bottom of his ear and he flinched.

"Fu—" he started, stopping himself when Sister Agnes moved past him. "What's your problem?"

"For your information, Dario," Cara said, not bothering to lower her voice. "May Phan is a horrible cocktease, so you can forget about getting into her panties." She pulled him away from the door and pointed down at the empty box. "Where's the little white box that was inside this one? It had the blue robe. We just had it altered. It's for my Mary's costume. We need it." When Dario tilted his head, looking lost, Cara inhaled as though it took everything in her not to scratch out his eyes. "The *Virgin* Mary? Blue for the Virgin, you *chooch*. The program is about great women in the bible, and Mary is the finale. We've already rehearsed Esther and Eve. Today we're doing Ruth, Sarah, and Mary. I *need* Mary's robe."

"Can't you just..." Dario swung his hand at Cara's uniform, pointing at her red collar before he shot a glance back toward the door. "I don't know... improvise?"

"You think the Virgin should wear red?"

"It's *just* a school program," Dario said, his gaze moving around the room when the small crowd of girls stopped to watch him.

"It's our *senior* program," Cara explained, her mouth tightening. "The Virgin can't wear red. Besides, I put the box in there myself. I *know* it was in there." She pointed to the box on the floor, stamping her foot.

Several of my sister's classmates hadn't returned to their jobs. They glared at Dario like he was clueless and insulting, so I stepped in, slapping a hand to his shoulder to quiet him before the asshole dug himself into too deep.

"Go check the car," I told him when Dario laughed at the frown still pulling down Cara's mouth.

Once Cara was in a mood, it lasted for-fucking-ever. I didn't need the headache, and I knew the sisters here didn't either. Cara shot Dario daggers as he went out the door.

I did my best to distract her, picking up the costumes and fabric to move them back into the box. "So, what about Ruth or Sarah? Can you dress either one of them now and practice while Dario looks for the missing costume?"

"We could," she said, tipping her chin at a younger girl carrying a box of programs to a table near the back of the room. "But the girl playing Sarah is home with the cramps. And our Ruth... Well..." Cara stopped, her eyebrows drawing together as she looked around the room. "I don't know what happened to her..."

"Who?" I asked, pulling out my Blackberry when it vibrated in my pocket. I was only half listening to my sister. I was more concerned with the phone number flashing across the screen. I'd called it before, many times, but being at St. Mary's and getting distracted by my kid sister and her friends had put me off my game.

"Did you hear me?" Cara asked when I slid my phone into my pocket.

"No, sorry, *rella*. Who are you looking for?"

She lowered her shoulders, grabbing the ribbon from my hand before she chucked it into the box.

"I said Sammy's missing. She's playing Ruth, and I thought she'd be back by now, but..."

A flash of Samantha Nicola's face shot to the front of my mind, and everything else went out of it—the girl calling me, Dario trying to fuck some cocktease, Cara and her bitchy attitude. When it came down to it, I was a hypocrite. I gave Dario shit for messing with a high school girl, when I'd been looking a little too hard at one all semester. If I was honest, I'd had my eye on her since we were kids—a girl that nobody on this planet could touch.

Cara didn't elaborate, and her silence pissed me off more than it should have. Hated that shit. Hated more that she went on ignoring me as I watched her. I copied her hand-motion and got her attention. "The fuck does that mean?"

"Johnny..." she whispered, rushing closer, her attention shooting around the room. "Oh my God, you can't say the F word in here."

"Tell me," I said, ignoring her. "What did you mean about Sammy? You thought she'd be back by now but...?"

Cara shrugged, nodding to two more girls who came into the auditorium. One was dressed in a costume made up of brown fabric secured around her head with a leather cord. "It's just that when Sammy does confession," Cara started, adjusting the girl's headpiece, "it typically takes forever." She stepped back, looking over the costume, tightening the belt before she glanced at me. "You know how she is. Niece of a priest. Heading for a convent after college. She's all...super... um...Catholic, I guess."

How could I not notice? It was respectable. Admirable how the girl kept herself focused. How serious she was when her uncle performed the mass and offered communion. Our papa and her uncle, Father Patrick, had been friends for a long time, and Sammy was always there, in the background, the small spot of color brightening everything gray around her.

I liked to tease her and had since she'd hit fifteen and the modest little dresses her uncle made her wear started fitting her curves tighter. She was still pious. Still gave nothing away, but when you looked at women as hard as I did, even high collars and hems hitting the knees couldn't hide much.

At seventeen herself, the shy, awkward, little girl Sammy had been was gone. She wasn't sweet and soft anymore. There were curves to her body now that I shouldn't have noticed but couldn't keep my attention from. There was a pout to her mouth that tempted and teased as her lips moved slowly in silent prayer. The girl did nothing to tempt me at all, and still, I found I couldn't keep from watching her, wanting her.

"She is," I finally agreed. "*Very* Catholic." I knew what I'd offer was a mistake before I made it. The words should have stayed in my mouth, where they belonged.

Sammy wasn't my friend. We were barely friendly to each other, but there had been long nights when her uncle came to visit Papa, when my father was feeling bad about one thing or another and needed his friend, not his priest, that Sammy got dragged along.

She pretended to read most visits, politely declining Cara's invites to go to parties or fund raisers my little sister organized for the museum our family owned. Opting instead to sit out in our courtyard with her nose in a book. I'd watch her, unable to keep myself from the temptation of her thick lips, oval face, exaggerated cheekbones, and the long, curled lashes that hit the tops of her cheeks as she read.

I'd try to pull her attention away from her books. She'd ignore me but still blushed like some wild fever had taken over her body. Until one August morning that I didn't flirt, and I suppose she'd expected it.

"Nothing inappropriate to say to me today?" she'd asked, not looking up from her book.

I couldn't fight the smile that pulled against my mouth. She'd noticed more than I'd given her credit for. Sammy was smart and shy, but she wasn't oblivious to my flirting.

"No, bella," I told her. "Not today." I'd leaned down into my chair, holding the crucifix around my neck between my fingertips. "Today, we remember my mama."

Even without looking at her, I knew Sammy was watching me. It was the first time she had. I liked the silence. Liked her attention even more.

8

"Was she beautiful like Cara?" she'd asked after a while, like that question was the simplest out of the bundle of many she had in her head.

"Yeah," I admitted, glancing at Sammy, unable to look away from those green eyes when I caught her gaze. "She was."

There was a second when Sammy studied me, pulling her bottom lip under her teeth like she wasn't sure if what she thought was stupid or if she should ignore me completely and get back to her book. But something in her eyes shifted, those light green flecks glinting as she watched me.

Sammy leaned toward me, pulling at the locket around her neck. "Mine was beautiful too," she said, showing me a picture inside the locket. She smelled like rosemary, and I caught a whiff of the scent from her hair when I moved closer to hold the locket and look down at the image. She wasn't wrong. The woman in the picture was beautiful—dark hair and olive skin like Sammy and a sharp, straight nose that matched hers. But the girl next to me had a square chin and tip at the end of her long nose, not angled like her mother's.

"She was beautiful," I finally told her, still holding the locket as I shifted my gaze to study her face. "Nowhere near as beautiful as you, though."

Then the blush returned to her face.

Never should have started that shit.

I knew better.

Sammy had a plan. She had a goal, and it didn't have a damn thing to do with me and the sinful armor I wore like a badge of dishonor.

Didn't seem ready to end it, no matter that I was eighteen and she wasn't. No matter that she would spend her life in the order, a bride of God.

I couldn't touch her.

But damn if I could keep away from her.

"If you're busy," I told my sister, pulling out my phone as a distraction. "I can go and find out what's keeping Sammy."

"Yeah," Cara said, her tone dismissive as another of her classmates stood in front of her, decked out in her costume, this one lavender and white. "Good luck. You can try to see if Father Patrick is still in the rectory. He might have seen her."

I nodded, still pretending to look at my phone as I turned to leave the room. It took five full minutes before I found Sammy, and after I did, there would be a few more dings in my armor.

For a while, I wore them proudly.

The library was empty when I found her. She had a spot; I knew that. I had caught her twice in the past month sitting in the farthest window seat in the darkest corner of the old library when I took calls I didn't think the good sisters of St. Mary's would appreciate hearing. The first time, Sammy had heard everything I said—every "fuck you" and "you son of a bitch!" Her cheeks had turned four shades of pink, and I'd spent a half hour trying to convince her I wasn't the devil sent to corrupt her.

Fuck that. Yes, I was.

The second time, she'd fallen asleep against the window during a storm as Cara sat for a makeup exam. I'd only agreed to keep an eye out for my kid sister while our papa was out of the country on business. He hated to miss her last month of school. He hated even more missing all the work she'd done on the exhibits and fund raisers she organized at the museum, practice for when she took it over after college, so I took up his slack.

Watching Sammy doze off against the window made up for the hours I'd spent lugging boxes of costumes and racks of chairs from the storage room to the gym. I'd tugged off my jacket and put it over her as she slept and just sat across from her, standing guard, though I didn't know why I'd done it. Aside from the fact that she was too damn beautiful to explain. Even more damn beautiful when she slept.

It wasn't hard to find her now.

Sammy had bent her long legs, her skirt draped over her knees as she faced the window and her arms curled tight together. Those huge green eyes were wide, unblinking, puffy, and red as she stared out of the glass. My stomach dropped as I watched. Some primitive drive hustled me closer to her as if I had some misplaced need to murder whoever made her cry.

"What's the matter?" I asked, the question coming out like a demand. "Who did this?"

For a shy, saintly girl, Sammy was cool. She didn't jump at my question. One slow glance in my direction and then she turned back toward the window. "You should go, Johnny Carelli."

Wasn't sure why that did something to me, her saying my full name like that, as though she liked the way all those letters moved around on her tongue.

Sammy didn't straighten when I sat on the window seat next to her. She didn't pull away from me either. She seemed too distracted by whatever had taken root in her head, like nothing else mattered but whatever it was that consumed her. There was a look in her eyes that seemed familiar to me, something that moved shadows around those green and hazel flecks in her irises. The longer I looked, the clearer the realization came of where I'd seen this expression before—in the mirror staring back at myself. It was guilt, plain and simple. But what on earth had someone like Sammy done to feel guilty about?

"Can I help?"

She shook her head, her lips pressed together, puckering the thick center. That did nothing to make her mouth seem smaller or her lips less tempting.

I inched closer, and this time, Sammy's shoulders tightened. "I'd kill anyone who made you cry or hurt you in any way."

"Why?"

It was an honest question, and I wasn't sure how to answer it. That day on the anniversary of my mother's death, Sammy had told me everything she knew about her mother. How she had only the stories her uncle told to fill in all the things she didn't know about the woman. I told her what I remembered of my mother. How sweet she'd been, how all those funny, warm memories I had of her got thinner the older I got.

That day out in our courtyard had been over a year ago. We weren't exactly strangers. There was something between us. It was the same hum of energy that kept me moving toward her every chance I got. But we didn't owe each other anything. No explanations. No excuses.

Didn't mean I could keep away from her.

Didn't mean I even wanted to try.

But I couldn't admit that to her. It would make no sense.

She had a plan. It was set. College. The order. Her future was waiting for her to get older, to get prepared. There was no room in her life for a distraction, and if I was anything to anyone, God knew it was a distraction.

Sammy watched me, those big green eyes open, unblinking, giving me the impression she wanted something from me she'd never admit. Something she knew I never would either, but she still clung to the hope I'd make a confession no priest could stomach hearing.

The look she gave me cut too deep. It was too much of a temptation.

I looked away from her, watching the courtyard below us through the window as I answered her. "I don't know, Sammy." I rested a palm next to hers on the cushion at her hip. "I just feel an intense need to..." From the corner of my eye, I caught her face when she opened her mouth, her wide, full lips parting, the bottom one glistening in the overhead light. I looked back to the window, spotting her expression, all breathless and curious. It was that reflection I stared at, unable to keep my attention from her, and the sweet hint of rosemary I caught coming from her hair.

"To...."

"To...protect you." I finally turned, moving another inch closer.

Sammy squeezed her eyes shut tight. The reaction was quick, like a twitch she couldn't control that made me hate myself just a little.

"You're scared of me."

"No....no," Sammy breathed, and even that sounded like a lie.

"You are." My voice came out in a strangle of sound, a little surprised, a hell of a lot disappointed that I could make her scared of me.

Our family was lower-level, but wealthy. That came with disputes, especially when my father hadn't chosen who he was loyal to or who would benefit more from his friendship. He was shrewd, but he couldn't keep anyone at arm's length for long, and staying neutral had cost him. There were *accidental* fires at his factories. There were *robberies* of his stores and shipments that got *lost*. It was a dangerous time to be a Carelli. But hell, I wasn't even twenty. No way my father would have me on the family payroll yet. Still, I was doing jobs. I'd set some assholes straight when my pops needed me to. I could hold my own. But shit, I wasn't a bruiser. I wasn't a roughneck asshole who got off on scaring the hell out of people. Sammy seeing me that way made my stomach burn like I'd gotten hold of something rotten at lunch.

I held my breath, trying to keep my cool as the worry shot up inside my chest. Sammy wouldn't look at me. Instead, she dropped her gaze to her folded hands in her lap as she mumbled through whatever it was she tried to get out. There were a few strands of hair slipping free from the barrette near her temple, and I had to stop myself from brushing it off her forehead.

Sammy inhaled, like she needed to calm herself before she spoke. "I'm...I'm scared of me...around you, Johnny," she admitted, speaking to her long fingers on her lap.

That rotten feeling in my gut shifted, moving lower, making my insides heat. The admission made me hard, had me wanting to pull her close, tug her onto my lap and show her just how scared she should be around me. But that wasn't what you did to a girl like Sammy Nicola. She was different. She was sweet, and I had a feeling I might be struck down just for thinking of touching her.

The image of my body sizzling from some supernatural lightning strike helped to cool me down, and I touched Sammy's hand, my fingertips gliding over that sweet, soft skin, up her arm, and to her neck until she lifted her head. "I would *never* hurt you."

"I think I know that."

I believed her. One look in those eyes told me enough that she believed what I said. I'd end myself before I did damage to her on purpose. Christ, but she was beautiful. Too good. Too perfect for the likes of me.

She didn't pull away when I touched her face, finally getting that hair off her forehead. "And I'd never let anyone else hurt you...not even yourself."

I knew guilt. I'd seen it in my own reflection too many times. And if I knew anything about Sammy, I knew there wasn't much she'd done in her life to feel guilty about. I shook my head and lowered my voice, hoping to calm her. "What are you scared of?"

Sammy moved her gaze away from my face, staring out of the window as I held her head still. When she spoke, her expression was a little dazed, a lot lost. "How...how you make me feel..." She regretted her words the second they were out as she bowed her head. The frown she gave me came quick. I didn't like it, liked even less how she pulled away, acted as though she didn't want to give up anything to me, especially not a confession about what I did to her.

"How's that?" I asked.

She tried moving off the window seat, shifting her legs away, but stopped when I held her hands, pulling her close. Sammy wouldn't look at me directly but kept her attention on the way I stroked my thumb over her wrist, like she couldn't get over how I touched her.

"Tell me," I said, knowing whatever she said would open a door I shouldn't walk through. "Please."

Her hands shook, like there was some current inside her she couldn't control. It made me want her more, made it impossible to walk away from her. I wanted to feel that current, wanted to let Sammy vibrate all around me.

She frowned as some debate happened inside her head, something that probably sounded like her uncle telling her what a sinner I was and how much damage I could do. That wasn't wrong, but I couldn't walk away. Not until I heard her truth. I had to hear what she wanted.

"Just tell me how I make you feel," I said, keeping my voice low and my touch steady.

Sammy exhaled, and I closed my eyes as the heat from her breath fanned against my neck. "Like...like I should feel ashamed for the things I imagine about you...and..." She blinked, licking her lips before she looked up at me. "You...and me."

Sammy was scared. That much I got from how the tremble from her hands had shifted to her lips. That soft, wet mouth I didn't seem able to stop staring at. We sat so close just then, watching each other, waiting, God knew for what. A pause, maybe? The next breath, the next move, the next noise that would make us spring into action.

She waited while I let her words shift in my head, reorganize, and become logic. Warnings flashed inside me, all of them sounding like my father's deep voice.

She wasn't for me.

She was off-limits.

She was too good.

She was innocent.

She was a saint's angel.

I was the devil's son.

This would not end well, but my God would it be fun while it lasted.

Sammy seemed to hold her breath. Those big eyes getting bigger when I moved my hand from her wrist and cupped her chin, rubbing a thumb along her skin. All I had to do was pull her close, take her mouth, end both our suffering. But first, God help me, I needed to tease her.

"Do you imagine kissing me?"

She froze, her mouth dropping open, gaze on my tongue when I moved it across my bottom lip.

"Touching me?"

Her attention stayed frozen on my mouth. Her breathing quickened, her fingers digging into my wrist as though she wasn't sure if she wanted to push my touch from her face or pull me closer.

I suppressed a smile as the sound of Sammy's throat working caught my attention when I moved closer to kiss her neck, whispering against her ear, "Tasting me?"

"Johnny," she whined when I pulled her close, running my mouth along her neck before I leaned back to watch her.

Sammy's mouth was inches from mine. She moved on the cushion in front of me, antsy and unsettled like she couldn't decide what to do with herself or how to be comfortable in her own skin. She held on to my collar when I kissed her once, a slow, soft kiss that left her panting.

"Tell me," I said, needing a confession. "I want you to admit it."

"All...all of it."

"Good," I said finally, rewarding Sammy's admission with another kiss, one that left me dizzy with how she gripped me.

Sammy pulled back, her breath in pants when I gripped her thigh, half lying across her with her leg over my hip. She was warm over me, that pleated skirt rising higher and higher. The soft, sweet breaths of hers coming closer the deeper I kissed her, the tighter she clung to me.

I could have taken her right there on that window seat. It wouldn't have taken a lot of effort. But one look and the low, amazed gasp from her when her skirt slipped higher and I grazed the front of her damp panties with a knuckle shook some sense into me. I pulled back, stopping only when Sammy's worried frown softened.

"*Oddio,* Johnny Carelli, I...I'm going to go to hell because of you."

I shrugged, my heart hammering in my chest when Sammy bit her lip again and fingered the top button of my shirt. Her surprise turned quickly to something that reminded me of open, primitive heat.

"Don't worry, *bella*," I told her, shifting our bodies to pull her close to me again, grinning at the low, soft moan she made when I slipped my hand underneath her skirt. I kept her face still, holding back a happy groan when she melted into my kiss. "I'll keep you company."

Chapter One

Johnny

Basilica of St. Mary's Cathedral - June 2007

The crowd was quiet but respectful. Even the man at the front of the room, holding his head high with a serious expression, was professional. I did not meet his eyes. I hadn't met anyone's eyes since walking in three hours ago.

There was too much emotion tied up in this day. Too many responsibilities that flooded me, that would soon consume me, to be distracted by the glare currently directed right at me.

Fuck him, I thought, relaxing against the plush cushion behind me, slipping my own scowl back to that asshole. Our gazes met, and I tightened my jaw, letting some of my frustration over this day filter out into my glare.

He had leveled a lot of blame at me over the years. It was time I sent some back.

Ahead of him, the children came, their voices low, somber. Then their song began, and the hymn filtered into the rafters, the echo of each note hitting the high ceilings above. I excused myself, torn by the memory of that song and what it had meant to me as a kid. What it meant to me as a man hearing it on this day, in this place.

I called off my guard and my sister as I moved through the crowd, ignoring the stares I got, bypassing well-wishers until I found myself alone. I was sufficiently secluded to let the emotion of the day peek out, just enough that I could breathe and not implode. I needed a release, some outlet that would distract me. Something that would keep me from screaming, cursing everyone in the room who did not feel what I did.

But there was no one. There was nothing.

There was only this sorrow and the blister of loss.

Or so I thought until I laid eyes on her.

The back row was empty and shaded in darkness. There were twenty minutes before it all began, and I had time, plenty of time, to find solace, some small semblance of peace alone in this spot. I would sit there, maybe, when the people moved through the doors, when the ushers cleared the aisle.

And then the group of nuns passed beyond the confessional.

Shock and surprise overwhelmed me.

Of course, she would be there. The children were hers. She guided them. They were her saving grace. They were her absolution for the sin I'd led her to. And the man, that glaring, angry man at the front of the church, he was hers as well. Duty. Honor. These were things that I had not made her forget with my mouth and my tongue, my touch and my taste.

Christ, she was such a temptation. Even now, sitting alone three rows from the back, her body rigid, her posture perfection. She was Sophia Loren made young again, brought into the twenty-first century to tempt and torture me just by being, existing. I could no more ignore her than I could disregard a da Vinci painting.

"You're a kid. You don't know what love is, Sammy. You need to forget about me."

I'd set flame to that perfect piece of art. Scorched it with a lie because I knew she was too perfect, too pure for me.

Even now, all these years later, I saw the look on her face—the devastated expression that told me I'd crushed her.

All that beauty fractured with one lie.

It broke her.

It destroyed me.

The last time I saw her had unhinged me. It had been years, but Sammy had still managed to devastate me with a look. The restaurant had gone silent as she'd faced me, looking perfect, looking fierce, all the rage and hatred of a decade fuming in those beautiful green eyes as she glared at me. Then, she slapped me right across the face.

But today, in this holy place, at this time, she should know I would find her. I was better prepared this time. I could wait. I could watch and see her pristine self. A perfect vision in her black dress and black hat, clutching her red rosary beads as she closed her eyes and prayed.

Not for me. No. Never. But maybe for Cara and her husband or the baby, my infant nephew. Maybe for our father, who'd never learned the truth of his son's greatest sin.

I moved, motioning to my bodyguard, Angelo, when he approached, motioning toward the rows where she sat, and I knew my man understood.

I wanted silence.

I wanted privacy.

Angelo would make sure that happened.

I slipped into the pew behind her, watching her profile, the long, closed lashes as they fell against her high cheekbones. They'd been dotted with tears the day I broke her heart.

"Why are you doing this, Johnny? I love you. I ache from how much I love you, and I...I could make you happy. I'd do anything to try."

We could be happy. We loved each other. We could be happy, but we'd never be safe. I knew that. Even as a kid, I knew that much.

Sammy's perfect, succulent mouth seemed to be in a perpetual pout, moving now in quick time as she muttered prayers under her breath.

"Hail Mary, full of grace..." I heard her pray.

The words pulled a smile from me, the only one I'd had today.

"My sister thanks you," I told her, looking forward, over the crowd, knowing she heard me.

Her prayer stopped, and Sammy tilted her head to the left. A silent acknowledgment that she knew I was behind her.

"And I thank you for your prayers," I told her.

"Your father was always very kind to me," she whispered.

I nodded, remembering how much my father thought of Sammy. How concerned he'd been when she'd chosen not to enter the order.

"And my uncle," she finished, pulling the smile from my face.

"You disgusting, vile, filthy boy! Taking advantage of my niece! Stealing her virtue!" her uncle had screamed at me long ago.

The old priest hadn't been wrong.

I had taken advantage of her.

I'd let her take advantage of me over and over again, but I couldn't make it right.

Not like he wanted me to.

Not like she wanted.

What kind of husband would I have been to her then? She was supposed to go to St. Agnes, go into the order, not become some capo's wife. In the end, money settled it. Money that wasn't mine, but money that kept the priest sated and Sammy off to a private college in Maine. But the priest hadn't let me go unshamed. He never told my father what happened, but he cursed me just the same.

"You are no son of this church, Johnny Carelli, and a bad Catholic. You shame your father's good name and your blessed mother's sweet soul."

I looked to the front of the church, spotting Sammy's uncle. Thankful his eyesight was too weakened with age, that it was likely he could not see me sitting so close to his niece. The old man might refuse to perform the service if he knew I spoke to Sammy.

"My father loved you both very much." I tightened my grip on the pew and leaned against it. "He thought highly of the work you do with the children and the..."

"What do you want?" Sammy no longer tilted her head toward me.

What did I want? What a loaded fucking question.

In a word? Her.

All of her.

Again.

Always.

I wanted a do-over.

I wanted her to see me and not be disgusted, but I knew that was a pipe dream. I'd settle for civility, but even that would likely be a stretch.

"Sammy..."

"Today is a sad day for our community, and I know you must be hurting." She turned her head, looking toward Cara sitting in the front pew closest to our father's casket, Kiel next to her, holding their baby. "Your sister will need your guidance and comfort. I would think you'd want to give her that today instead of trying to torment me."

"Torment?" My voice cracked.

At that, she turned, gaze moving up to look at me. "It's what you are best at."

A flood of memories came back to me. A thousand lost moments I held deep inside my heart when I needed them. Sammy's head bent in prayer the day I first saw her, wearing a white dress and gloves as she knelt on the prayer bench and black streaks stained her perfect face.

Then later, years later, that day in the library, her breath heavy, her bottom lip wet, plump like a grape on the vine, her scent fresh, hot as I leaned closer, wanting her so much, having her want me, but knowing it was a sin.

God, how I'd wanted to be a sinner that night.

"You should leave," she said, pulling me from my memories, reminding me where I was and why.

"I will," I told her, tired of the distance that my guilt and her anger had put between us.

Her uncle was old and mean. He'd be dead soon, and Sammy would be left with only her grief and rage. If I didn't intercede, there would be nothing left of her but bitterness. I knew firsthand she held too much fire for that to happen.

"On one condition."

"I don't need to meet your conditions," she said, not bothering to look my way when she answered.

I sent Angelo a grateful smile. It was a blessing to have such diligent staff. He unraveled every secret, gave me every advantage I needed. "Your lease is up next month on the children's center, correct?"

Sammy jerked around, finally showing me her full face, more beautiful than I remembered. Even more striking than it had been when she screamed at me on the street outside Così Buono weeks ago. "What did you do?"

I leaned forward just to get a whiff of her scent. It had been too long. "Trying to make amends."

She stiffened when I reached for her, my courage failing me when Sammy squeezed her eyes shut as though the idea of my touch would be torture.

"Believe it or not," I told her, leaning back against the pew again. "I'm trying to help." I pulled out a card from my jacket pocket, offering it to her as the choir at the front of the church began to sing another hymn, this one calling congregants to their seats. "We have a lot to discuss. When this is over."

She didn't take the card, just stared down at it.

I placed it on the pew next to her leg before standing, offering a nod to my sister when she turned in her seat, her gaze searching for me. "Thank you again,

Sammy, for paying your respects. It's always good to see you."

"I wish I could say the same."

I leaned down, grinning when she looked away from me. "Don't worry, *amore mia*. You will one day very soon."

Chapter Two

Sammy

Parasites are bloodsuckers. They latch on to you, sinking beneath the surface of who you are, and hold tight. They don't loosen their grip. They don't allow any separation from the host until they've gotten their bellies full or their needs met.

The particular parasite wrecking my life was the most dangerous kind. He came in a well-constructed package—chiseled cheekbones and full lips, a perfect, straight nose, and dark, impossibly black eyes. Strong, supple shoulders and strength in every movement. Worst of all, my little parasite had a mission, one he didn't seem eager to relinquish... Me.

Johnny Carelli came with my uncle's job. He was the legacy of the man Uncle Patrick considered a dear friend, and I had stupidly been duped by his smile and charm.

As a naïve kid, I'd fancied myself in love with him. Back then, I'd convinced myself I'd never feel that way about anyone else in the world, and then, not long after he'd wrecked me, I did.

Over a decade later and I was still seeing shades of that bastard everywhere I looked.

"Your uncle called," Indra said, slipping into my office with her arms weighed down with a stack of bright-green T-shirts. She laid the bundle on the corner of my desk before she flopped into the chair next to the door. "For the third time. What gives?"

"He found out Johnny talked to me at the funeral."

Indra sat up, her dark eyebrows curling up her forehead until they disappeared behind the bangs that fell into her black eyes. "*The* Johnny? Not the one who..."

"The same one," I said, waving a hand to silence her before she started asking for details. Indra always wanted details. "And before you start, he was just trying to mess with my head. He owns this building."

She opened her mouth, her eyes widening further, but she didn't ask whatever question bubbled on the tip of her tongue.

I leaned on my elbows, slumping against the desk. "He was teasing me like he always does. He's working an angle. He's always got an angle. When I find out what it is, I'll tell him no, maybe smack him across the face again like I did a few weeks back. And then he'll get bored and be off harassing some other poor woman."

"But, Sammy..." Indra had the same look on her face she got when she was working a theory. Those never led me anywhere good. That look, in fact, frequently led to tequila nights at some karaoke bar in Chinatown with Indra screaming Alanis Morrisette at the top of her lungs and ended with me holding back her thick hair while she puked in a toilet. "What if he's genuinely sorry about you and all that...stuff." I cocked an eyebrow at her, not bothering to lower it until she made that ridiculous grin leave her mouth. "I'm just saying. People change."

"People can change," I told her, picking up a few of the T-shirts as a distraction. "But Johnny Carelli is not 'people.'"

She fiddled with the collar of her striped button-up as she watched me closely, her attention sharp and penetrating. She was always looking me over, watching for slips and cracks in the veneer she swore I wore. But there was nothing around me except for the tightly constructed wall time and discipline had created. Johnny had begun to lay the first bricks. I finished the rest the longer the hurt he left inside me grew. My defense was solid by now. Nothing would crack it.

"So, if he's not people, then what is he?" she asked, still watching me.

"Proof that I'm not perfect."

"That's not proof. Besides, I don't believe that for a second." Indra stood, stretching her arms over her head before she turned to leave. A small sliver of brown skin peeked between her untucked shirt and her fitted designer jeans she likely picked up at a consignment shop. "Well, Miss Not-So-Perfect, call your uncle. I'm tired of taking his messages. He already thinks I'm corrupting you with my bad Indian juju."

"He does not."

"Sammy, he sends me a book of novenas and rosary beads every year for Christmas."

"He sends everyone the same gift," I said, folding the shirts into a small pile that I stuffed on top of my filing cabinet. "He's just being polite."

"Every year for six years, even though he knows I'm a Hindu and don't celebrate Christmas?"

"He's senile?" I tried, laughing when Indra rolled her eyes.

"He's petty," she shot back.

"That," I told her, not holding back a laugh, "I can't deny..."

We both toward the crashing sound that came from the hallway outside of my office. There was the twist of metal and a booming rattle, followed immediately by the thunder of running feet and the screaming voices of our kids. Indra and I darted from my office and made it to the activity room just as the double doors flew open and students from both of the afternoon summer classes descended. Thirty or forty preteens ran straight for us, screaming about the falling ductwork crashing to the floor.

"Calm down," I tried as a few of the volunteers organized the kids into groups.

Indra followed me into the large activity room, both of us stopping short. My stomach dropped when I spotted the panels from the ceiling lying on the floor, along with several feet of ductwork. "Shit," I whispered, wondering how the hell this had happened. I pulled out my cell, thumbing through the contacts until I found the contact for Mike, the super, but I stopped scrolling when I heard Indra's small laugh at my left. "What?"

"Ten minutes ago, you said Johnny owns the building."

"Yeah? And?"

"And...Mike told you two weeks ago he'd be on a cruise for most of June. It's on your calendar." She grabbed my phone, scrolling herself, but she didn't seem to find the number she looked for.

"He's not in there."

"Well, you need to find his number, boss." Indra looked over the damage in disbelief. "Because this is one time you might have to take advantage of whatever angle that man is working."

Chapter Three

Johnny

Everything about Sammy told me she wasn't here to impress me. From the way she curled her arms tight to her body as she waited inside my office, her chin lifted, still wearing her sunglasses, to the casual jeans and black spaghetti-strap shirt she wore. But even that, she managed to make look classy.

I stood observing her just outside my office, watching Sammy stare out of the large window next to my desk. I needed a second to get my head together. It was a surprise that she showed. I never expected her to. But there she was, stepping out of the hot June temperatures in jeans, a thin black shirt, black heels, and that devastating face like she was ready for the fucking runway and not some run-down community center that needed a complete overhaul.

"Sir? Can I get you and Miss Nicola something to drink?" my assistant asked.

"No," I told Nadine. "Just hold my calls." I straightened my tie before walking through the doorway and closing the door behind me. I'd hoped Sammy would relax when she saw me. I'd hoped she'd at least lose her glasses and return my smile when I greeted her, but she'd spent a long time hating me. Didn't much matter what I'd hoped for.

"Sammy," I said, deciding not to offer her my hand. Stubborn woman wouldn't take it, that much I knew. I sat, grateful she couldn't see how I couldn't keep my foot from bouncing under my desk as she sat across from me, slowly slipping her glasses off her nose and into her bag without moving her gaze from my face.

The woman was stone-cold, and that shit had me forgetting who I was.

She kept her mouth tight, unsmiling, arms still folded like she'd caught a chill standing in my office waiting for me. I noticed how her hair had started to stick to her temples. It was hot for June, and she hadn't been in the building that long. "Can I get you..." Sammy shook her head once, and I didn't bother finishing my offer. "Fine," I said, folding my fingers together. "What can I do for you?"

Finally, she rested against the chair, moving her hands on the arms of the chair before she gripped them, her nails turning like claws into the fabric. "There was an accident today at the center."

I sat up, ignoring the dip of tension I felt move between my eyebrows. "Was anyone hurt?"

"Everyone is fine, but some of the ductwork fell onto the main activity room floor where the children were rehearsing. They're performing for Bishop Wilkens next week at St. Anthony's. I sent the children home, and my uncle says we can use the basilica for the next week. But that's only temporary." Sammy's nails dug deeper into the chair, and I exhaled.

This wasn't easy for her, I knew that. I couldn't be an asshole here. I wanted to help her. It was the least I could do, and I did myself no favors by making her ask me for what I already knew she wanted.

"Sammy, I've already got a crew on standby. I wanted to give you some time to adjust to the news of my ownership before any work was done. But I don't want anyone in danger, especially not your kids."

She looked away from me, and I didn't know what to make of the expression she hurried to push off her face. Whatever it was, Sammy recovered, nodding for me to continue.

"If you can't use your uncle's church for the next few months, is there another place available for the programs?"

"No," she said, her frown returning. "We'd have to organize the work one project at a time."

"Hmm." I leaned back in my chair, not liking the idea of such slow progress. "It would make more sense to knock it all out at once."

"Not an option," she said, folding her arms again.

There was a tone in her voice that reminded me of the girl I used to know. Not the woman who rattled me outside of the restaurant or the pissed-off lady at my father's funeral a few days ago. Some hint in her tone brought back the memory of the Sammy I knew before things got out of hand. Before I let everything go too far.

"You don't know a lot about compromise, do you?" I asked.

She arched an eyebrow, the small expression a challenge. "There's no need for me to compromise. This isn't a negotiation."

"It's not?"

"No," she said, relaxing again, like she had inside information I didn't and the idea of that made her happy. "It's definitely not."

"I don't think you appreciate..."

"No, Mr. Carelli," she started, putting out a hand to shut me up.

Huh.

Nobody did that shit. Not ever.

Once, Ricky Marconi interrupted me in a meeting, and I glared at him for doing it. That asshole spent the next six weeks in Newark at the docks loading trucks because he pissed me off and then three more months at my little cousin Smoke's factory outside of White Plains. Then he cleaned the toilets of a strip club just to learn his lesson. No one interrupted me. Ever. So why the hell was I giving Sammy a pass?

"What you don't appreciate," she continued, ignoring the way I sat there staring at her, unable to keep my mouth from hanging open, "is that you are legally obligated, as owner, to maintain the structural integrity of the building." She grabbed her bag, thumbing through an envelope inside before she extracted a thick bundle of papers and handed it over to me. "The terms of my lease are clear. This is a copy in case you don't have access to Mike's records since he's out of town."

I glanced at her, looking over the sheaf of papers, trying to keep my expression neutral, but Sammy could read me. That much hadn't changed in the past decade. No one could call me on my bullshit better than her. When I looked away from her, not giving away the fact that I had no clue who she was talking about, Sammy let a quick twitch move the side of her mouth.

"Thought so," she said, crossing her leg.

"What?"

"What was your plan?" Her tone was light, but there was an edge to it that could cut steel. Sammy may be beautiful, she may have a sweet, gentle way about her, something that came through her eyes when she smiled, but it was all bullshit.

If you were her enemy, if she hated you, you'd never know it. Not until she had you by the balls and was already closing her fist around you.

"You thought you'd interrupt my life, take over my lease, buy out the building, and what? Get on my good side by fixing it up? Throw some paint on the walls, maybe hang a few pictures?" When I dropped the rental agreement on the desk and leaned against my armrest, ready to explain myself, Sammy shook her head, already stopping whatever excuse I had before I could offer it up. "The center, those kids? You don't mess with them. You don't get to mess with my life like that, Johnny Carelli. That place is the only good some of those kids have. So, if you're going to jump in with a plan to mess with that, I'm here to let you know, I'll make you miserable."

"That's not what I want," I tried, shaking the agreement in my hand when she tried to argue. "I know what this means to you."

"You have no idea what anything means to me."

The air cooled at her words. Just like that, with the statement Sammy seemed convinced of, she made it clear we'd fallen off topic. She thought I didn't know her. She thought I had no idea who she was or what made her happy anymore.

Maybe she was right. Maybe I would never make amends for hurting her, for destroying the innocent girl she'd been. But I promised myself right then, I'd do everything I could to never stop trying.

She seemed to realize how much she'd admitted the second her voice lifted, and a small glimpse of anger showed with her words. But Sammy, being the cool, calm woman she was, recovered, shifting in her seat, chin moving up before she looked me squarely in the eyes with an expression that begged me to challenge her.

I chose not to gamble.

I chose, in that moment, to play the peacemaker.

My movements slow, I leaned forward on my elbows, folding my fingers together before I looked up at her and released a long exhale. "Till I'm an old man, Samantha, I'll apologize to you. Every day, with every breath, so you know I mean it."

There was a small shift in her features, moving the quick surprise off her face the second it had appeared, and then Sammy recovered, shaking her head. "I don't need your apologies." She cleared her throat, looking to the window as she spoke. "I need you to know that Mike is the super, and he's on a cruise. I need you to know that the ductwork fell, and we need it repaired. The furnace doesn't work either, and only the bathrooms on the second floor function properly." She turned to look at me, narrowing her eyes with a pause, then nodded to the pen next to my hand, giving me a silent command that had the right side of my mouth quirking.

I followed her order but hid the grin before she could spot it. I'd let her bark orders at me. At least she was talking to me.

Once I'd started writing the list of repairs she'd mentioned, Sammy continued. "The bathroom situation is a problem, considering our classes are on the fourth floor. We have a kitchen, but only one working burner, which makes it hard to provide hot meals for the kids who probably don't get much to eat at home anyway." She glanced at my list, then to my face to frown at me before she continued. "The tile on the floor of the activity room is broken or breaking, and I'm pretty sure the entire place is coated in lead paint. It needs a lot of work, and that takes a lot of money. That's not something I have on hand, and donations and fund raisers don't happen a lot during the summer because most people disappear from the city when their kids are out of school."

I nodded, finishing the list before I set the pen down. I looked back up at that beautiful face, making sure I didn't smile and didn't give her any expression other than something that passed for acceptance. I'd give her what she wanted, then I'd ask for what I needed. "I'll take care of it."

"You'll... I don't..." She shook her head, then inhaled again. "You can't just..." Sammy turned her head and watched me as though she wasn't sure if I was trying to play her. I wasn't, but she was cunning. She was smart, and from what Cara had told me, Sammy wasn't easily swayed by anyone. "That will take a lot of..."

"You need it taken care of?"

She nodded, her frown not disappearing.

I waved off her nod. "I'm the building owner, like you said. I'll handle it."

Sammy waited a full minute, watching me and sizing me up. Her attention was sharp as she stared at me before she finally spoke. "And you'll help me find a temporary rehearsal spot?"

I thought about it, wondering if Cara still owned the building downtown for storage or if our cousin Antonia still needed renters for the shop a few blocks from Sammy's center. "Yeah, I think I can find something. I'll make some calls."

"And..." she started, that curious, doubtful expression not fracturing an inch, "you'll make sure my uncle doesn't find out you're helping?"

That one had me pausing. I grinned, earning a glare from Sammy I guessed she'd had waiting. "How long can the man go on hating me?"

She sat up straighter, and some of that calm control slipped from her. "He's always going to hate you."

I relaxed against my chair, laughing at her somber expression. "He's a priest."

"He's not perfect."

Father Patrick hating me was something I'd gotten used to years ago. I'd paid the man. I'd donated and handed over hush money to him and his church whenever they asked. Then I stopped when I realized the old bastard was counting on perpetual Catholic guilt to bleed me dry forever. That shit ended when I realized I'd never be forgiven for my sins. Not by him.

But I didn't care what the old man thought of me. I didn't care if he knew I was the one helping Sammy with her center and her charity. Besides, this might help me with a few problems I needed resolved and get me closer to her at the same time.

Her gaze was sharp and followed my movements as I rubbed my chin, considering her request. I cocked my head, pretending to really give the whole clusterfuck my full attention before I made a decision. "Fine, then," I started, straightening in my chair and adjusting my jacket and tie, ready to negotiate even if Sammy wasn't. "The renovations and any financial assistance you need are a given. I've obligated myself to this charity, and I want to help."

"Out of the goodness of your black heart?"

"Because I owe you." I meant that shit, even if she didn't believe me. I made sure there wasn't even a hint of a grin or the smallest smirk on my face so she knew that. "It's for you and only you."

"Damn it, Johnny. You've got a condition." Sammy flopped back against her chair, shoulders slumping for the first time. She cringed when I didn't hold back the wide, toothy smile I gave her. She shook her head, muttering under her breath. "I knew it."

"This promise of keeping your uncle from knowing..."

"Johnny..."

"I can agree to that, but I need *something* from you." Her hair was pulled back, but it moved against her shoulder when she jerked her gaze up at me, a sharp, angry glare shooting in my direction that had me laughing already. She had the same pissed-off death glare now that she'd had at seventeen. Her mind was in the gutter, that much I could tell. Sammy thought I was only concerned with one thing because I pretty much had been as a kid. She swore I didn't know what she wanted, but by the way she sat up straight, tugging up her shirt to cover her cleavage, I guessed she probably thought what I wanted from her was something I could get from any woman.

"Ah, *bella*, not that the thought hasn't crossed my mind a thousand times, but no, I do have some dignity. I'm not going to blackmail you into sleeping with me."

Sammy moved her shoulders, releasing a half chuckle that told me she didn't believe me for a second.

I didn't bother trying to convince her, though I did make her a promise I had every intention of keeping. "Sammy, the next time I see you naked, it will because you want it, because you can't keep from touching me. And trust me, I won't have to do any convincing or conniving to get you undressed."

Finally, Sammy laughed, the sound loud and from her belly. It was the first time in the half hour she'd been in my office that I believed she finally relaxed. She looked beautiful, more beautiful than I'd seen any woman look in a long damn time. Sammy laughed over my promise like I was out of my head. "You're an arrogant bastard, Johnny Carelli."

"Absolutely."

After several minutes, Sammy's laughter died, and she settled back against her chair. "Go on, then. Tell me what you want from me."

One slow look over her face, down her body, which she ignored, and then I finally spoke. "There is an account I am trying to secure—" I stopped whatever sarcastic comment Sammy seemed ready to make when she opened her mouth with a shake of my head "—for my private business not affiliated with my father's companies." Knowing Sammy, she probably didn't believe any of my businesses were legitimate. My father was into private gambling, *finding* goods when they *fell* off trucks, and *cleaning* money. He'd never messed with drugs or prostitution but had owned several strip clubs and wasn't always purely honest with his taxes. I made sure those businesses stayed up and running, but I also ran several IT and security companies, one of which I was trying to get off the ground. Which was why I needed Sammy.

"I have several dinner meetings arranged with a potential investor. They're friendly, family-style meals. He has a wife and children. I do not, and that's a sticking point. I don't have time to track down a girlfriend or find someone..."

"You mean," she started, crossing her leg to turn her chair. She looked a little too smug, and the half grin on her face irritated me more than it should have. Also made me a little hard. "You have to pretend to be a respectable man for this legitimate businessman, and the escorts you normally use aren't appropriate to act as your girlfriend?"

I considered her a moment, thinking she'd played me. The woman was good at negotiation. That teasing little smirk would have any man handing over his checkbook in a heartbeat. Biting the inside of my lip, I kept my cool, head moving in a slow nod. "I want to make an impression."

"And I'll help with that?"

"Samantha, you're intelligent, funny, charming, and the single most beautiful woman I've ever seen in my life. You *are* the impression." I caught her gaze, took a second to watch her, see if her green eyes were still light or if the years had darkened them.

She looked back at me, and I could have sworn she wasn't breathing.

There was no smirk on her face. No frown that told me she was pissed I'd tried buttering her up. Just then, between the low, soft sound of the vents kicking on and the muted ring of Nadine's phone from outside my closed door, there was only Sammy and me, watching each other with the shadow of what happened between us thickening the air around us. I could almost taste her. I could almost remember how warm her skin had been.

Then, just like that, the moment ended. Sammy blinked, breaking the silence with a laugh that sounded forced. "You know, for a second there, I almost believed you."

"It wasn't a line." I picked up the pen, gripping it between my index finger and thumb to give me something to hold on to. Sammy turned toward the window, answering me with her attention on the early afternoon skyline to our left. "If you say so."

Her profile was perfect, everything about her flawless, still like some starlet from the fifties frozen in time, a woman no other woman around her could hope to measure up to. Funny thing was, Sammy had no clue just how beautiful, how intimidating she was.

"Fine," she said finally, still not looking at me. "Have the crews start next week after you find us a suitable place to hold summer classes and rehearsals until the building's ready." She slipped a business card from her purse and put it on my desk. She stood from her chair with her bag clutched in front of her, as though that would keep me from getting too close when I circled my desk and stood in front of her. "If you keep your word and my uncle doesn't find out, I'll go with you to your dinners. Text me with the dates and times. But don't get any ideas."

I stood quickly, and the movement made Sammy flinch, as if she expected me to touch her face. "All I have left are ideas about you, Sammy."

She turned, hurrying to the door, but I took hold of the doorknob before she could grab it. She stood in front of it, waiting for me to let her out, then glanced up at me when I didn't.

"They're really good ideas too." When I leaned forward, taking her wrist with my free hand, Sammy didn't object. "You might like the ideas I have."

She watched me as I kissed her hand, not taking my attention from her gaze, savoring the warm feel of her skin and the still sweet smell that lingered there. Sammy looked me over, head tilting as though I were a kid who'd only understand her if she spoke in short, slow sentences. "You keep your ideas, Johnny Carelli. They're the closest you'll get to having me naked again. That much, I promise you."

Sammy slapped my hand from the doorknob and was out of my office before I could respond. She left me with nothing but the sweet smell of her skin, and a laugh caught in my throat that stayed there all afternoon.

Chapter Four
Sammy

I knew better than to drink so much wine. Especially in front of strangers. It made me a bit too friendly. A lot too forgetful.

"Another glass, Samantha?" Mrs. Garcia was already refilling my glass before I could refuse.

"Oh no. Thank you, though."

"I insist. You have a driver, yes? Your man Johnny says you take a driver because you both like to drink red on Friday nights. Here, have another." The beautiful Spanish woman poured an entire glass full, and I tried to keep my eyes from bulging.

"*Oddio*," I whispered, trying to keep the glass from spilling when the woman pushed it in front of me. "Thank you."

"Is that four or five?" Johnny asked, leaning over the back of my chair to speak next to my ear. I suppressed a shiver. Something I doubted he missed, and I ignored the pleased laugh he released when I waved him away. "What?" he asked.

"Mind your business."

"Men are so nosy, aren't they?" Mrs. Garcia said, sitting back down across the table next to her husband. "This one is always asking me where I've gone, what I do when he's at the office." She pushed her husband away when he wrapped a large arm around her shoulder, his attention on her face as she spoke. Three hours with this couple and already I could tell they were still smitten after ten years of marriage. "I tell him always, I'm busy. I have children and charities, I take classes, and care for my *mamá*. You worry about yourself, I tell him. And he's always 'But, *mi amor,* how did you spend your day? Did you miss me?' Always 'Did you miss me?' Ah!"

"It's because I *do* miss you, *amado*." Mr. Garcia was a middle-aged man nearing fifty with salt-and-pepper hair and small lines around his eyes. This was his first marriage, the couple had informed us, and he had met his wife, who was several years younger than him, at her Costa Rican hometown library in San José where she had worked as the head librarian. He'd visited every day for a week while he vacationed there, trying to get her to agree to a date.

"Well, I think it's sweet," I told Mrs. Garcia, smiling when she blushed at the attention her husband gave her.

She called the man off again, hiding a grin behind the long drink she took from her wine. She patted his hand when he squeezed her shoulder, then seemed to notice the way Johnny and I watched the couple. "Johnny," the woman started. "Tell us, how did you meet Samantha. Was it love at first sight?"

"Yes. You must tell us, *por favor,*" Mr. Garcia said, pulling his attention away from his wife, now seeming interested in his guests. He and Johnny had spent an hour discussing the new security business Johnny wanted to start, going over projections and business plans, but the more wine Mr. Garcia drank, the more he seemed bored of business discussions. The Garcias were already affectionate. Wine only added to that.

Johnny slipped his arm along the back of my chair, and I did my best not to flinch away from his attention. It was a weird sensation, being this close to him, trying to separate all the years of reminding myself what a horrible person he was, of all the terrible things he'd said and done to me, and the sweet boy he'd once been. The man he was now was different from both, and I didn't know what to think. I only knew I'd made him a promise. I'd play this part, and he'd help me with the center and keep my uncle out of the loop.

It would test my acting skills.

"That's a long story," I tried, holding the wineglass as a distraction.

"Not very long," Johnny said, squeezing my shoulder. "Our families have known each other for years. We fell in love when we were kids, and then...I broke her heart." When I jerked a gaze at him with the glass still in my hand, he pulled it away with his attention on my face as though he were worried I'd throw my wine in his face. "I blew it," he told the Garcias, still watching me. "And by the grace of God, Sammy decided to give me a second chance. She's letting me make up for all the terrible things I did to her when I was a stupid kid."

I couldn't speak. In the back of my mind, I knew this was all make-believe. Johnny Carelli had no intention of making anything up to me. His guilt still weighed on him; I understood that. But this? Pretending that he'd loved me? Making me believe that he wanted another chance? That was a show, and he was damn convincing with his performance.

Across the table, I could make out the small exchanges the married couple had with each other, but I couldn't stop watching Johnny's expression. How his eyes, shining and slightly bloodshot from the wine, sparkled in the candlelight flickering all over the table, made his handsome face seem unreal.

"*Besala.*" I heard, blinking when the laughter picked up and Johnny looked away from me.

"What?" he asked Mr. Garcia.

"Kiss her." He motioned between the two of us. "*Amigo*, a woman that lovely looks at you the way your *corazón* just did when you say such a thing, you must kiss her."

"I don't..." I started, blinking back the fog brought on by the small moment and the numbing look Johnny gave me.

"Well, if you insist," Johnny said, turning toward me. He held my face, whispering low against my mouth. "I'll owe you, Sammy. Just play along."

He moved in slowly, angling my head, hovering over my mouth. With my eyes open, I could only watch as he descended as though he expected me to push him away. When I didn't, Johnny dropped one soft kiss on my mouth with enough pressure that our lips barely touched before the weight of his fingers tightened. This time, the kiss lasted longer, was a deeper tease with mouth and tongue stroking, playing, touching together, his control so certain, possessive, until I forgot who and where I was. Who he was and why we were together in this place, performing such a desperate act for these strangers.

Johnny's low rumble of pleasure moved up his throat—half moan, half growl—and he angled away from me, still holding my head in his hands, pressing one last small kiss on my mouth before he opened his eyes to look at me again.

"There," he said, his voice a gravel road of sound. "Was that so terrible?"

"Not...not so bad."

And, I hated to admit, it wasn't.

I tried to tell myself the wine caused all the fuzzy-headed thoughts. It was responsible for the giggling I'd shared with Mrs. Garcia when she conveyed how she almost got pregnant again just watching Johnny kiss me at her dining room table. I told myself, as his driver sped through the city toward my apartment, that I hadn't enjoyed the kiss more than I had all those secret, sweet kisses Johnny had stolen from me as a kid.

It was just the wine.

But one thought kept creeping into my subconscious as the Manhattan streets flew past us and Johnny kept talking about Mr. Garcia's excitement over the prospect of this new business.

Johnny Carelli was a better kisser than he had been ten years ago.

"Of course, we've all had a little bit of wine..."

"We all did," I offered, not paying attention when Johnny went silent. Not until I felt the pressure of his hand against mine on the armrest. I turned, looking down to see how close Johnny sat to me in the car, then stared back up at him. "Date's over."

He nodded but didn't move his hand.

"And my apartment is three blocks away."

Again, he nodded. But this time, he leaned forward, reaching a hand toward me.

I stopped him, grabbing his wrist. "We aren't acting anymore, Johnny."

He paused half a second longer than it took to smile, then any traces of cool left his features. "Who says I was acting?"

This was Johnny Carelli being his best authentic self. I'd seen it before, years ago and then again the day of his father's funeral. When he meant something, when the truth came from him, it was all there in his eyes. Just then, he wanted me to know he wasn't playing a part.

My heart thundered, overtaken by the sensation of blood pumping in my veins as irritation coursed through me. Was he playing me? Using the Garcias and this dinner as a way to get me back somehow? Did he think I could ever forget what he did or the damage he left behind? Or who he was outside of the legitimate businesses he ran?

"I was," I told him, moving against the door. "My Lord, Johnny, what are you thinking?" I watched him, unsurprised when his expression didn't change. He was so stubborn, always had been. "Is this the game you're playing? You want to manipulate me to, what? Win me back? Get me on my back again?"

"No, Sammy. Why would you think that?" He sat up and his expression hardened. "How can you think that?"

"Because you have no honor."

His mouth dropped open, and Johnny flinched. I hadn't planned to say the words. They slipped out before I'd given them any real consideration, but the slip was enough. They were the truth. He'd taken more than I'd offered, and he'd never looked back. Johnny would never understand, could never understand, what a mess he left behind when he broke my heart.

"I'm not..." He nodded once, and his shoulders drooping as though something weighing a ton had just been dropped on his back. The car pulled to the curb and then stopped, and before I had a chance to register that we were outside my building, Johnny was out of the car and slipping around to my side to open the door for me.

I stepped out of the car, letting him take my elbow to help me into my building, and we didn't speak as we went inside. I nodded to the night guard as we waited at the elevators. Johnny tightened his features, his mouth drawn down and a severe line forming between his eyebrows. He kept his distance, standing across from me, hands behind his back as though he didn't want me to think he would try to make a move.

But that hard expression did more than make him look severe and irritated. It worked a knot in my stomach. One that grew thicker and heavier as the elevator doors opened and Johnny ushered me inside. He wouldn't ask to come into my apartment. He hadn't asked to come inside when he'd picked me up. And that knot was my own good upbringing weighing me down, telling me that I'd managed to hurt his feelings by speaking the truth.

Damn it.

I shouldn't feel bad about this.

But I did.

He leaned against one side of the car, looking up at the numbers as they grew higher and higher. The hard set of his features not relaxing.

I couldn't take the silence another second longer. "You...weren't all bad," I tried, watching him from the corner of my eye, trying to keep from smiling when I spotted him glancing down at me. "You got May Phan the pregnancy test that summer when your cousin Dario thought he knocked her up."

Johnny suppressed a snort. "Lot of good it did him."

"Because the baby wasn't his?"

"Even May didn't know whose baby that was." He moved closer, slipping both hands into his pockets. "It was nothing," he tried, looking away from me.

"You look out for your family. That...that takes honor."

"No, Sammy," he said, standing in front of me. "That's loyalty." Johnny stared at the floor as though he couldn't make himself look at me directly when he admitted the truth. "You weren't wrong. I had no honor. What I did to you..."

"Johnny..."

"I mean it." He leaned a hand on the wall next to my head, and I caught the faint hint of his cologne, the smell bringing forward a thousand memories I'd tried to suppress for years. "I am sorry. I mean it. I'm sorrier than I can say."

One look at his face and I thought he might mean it. There wasn't any humor in his expression. No smirk or twitching laughter on his mouth that made me think he was pretending. Johnny meant it. And if he meant this, he must have meant that kiss from earlier.

My heartbeat doubled for a different reason, and I decided to change the subject. I was grateful when the elevator slowed, opening on my floor.

"You really weren't as bad as I say," I said, walking out of the car and down my hall, tugging my bag open to grab my keys.

"No?" he asked, keeping step with me.

"No. I guess I'd say there were three things that made me go a little stupid over you," I admitted, stopping at my door. I put the key into the dead bolt and turned to face him, but I didn't unlatch the locks.

"Well, now you have to tell me, *bella*."

I quirked my mouth, pretending to debate his request before I sighed, as though his demand were ridiculous. "Fine, if you have to know, it was your laugh."

"My laugh?"

"Yes. It's a good laugh. Belly deep. I like an honest laugh when you're not afraid to let the world know you think something's funny. When you don't care who knows you love to laugh. That's the kind of laugh you have, Johnny."

"Huh," he said, leaning on an elbow against the wall to look down at me. "I've been paid a compliment or two before by women, but none of them have ever mentioned my laugh."

"That's because they were trying to flatter you." I straightened, putting distance between us. "I'm not."

"No?"

"Why would I? We have a business arrangement. Nothing more."

I expected him to frown, maybe grow sullen and irritated again, but Johnny didn't stop smiling, moving in closer and taking my hand. "We can see each other for other things aside from these dinners with the Garcias."

"Or we can stick to the arrangement."

"Or..."

"No 'ors,' Carelli." I stepped back, turning the knob, but Johnny stopped me, grabbing my hand to kiss my knuckles.

"You're gonna let me take you out on a date. A real one, not part of our 'negotiation.'"

"No," I said and pulled my hand free. "Never."

I stepped inside, taking my keys out of the lock. I nearly had my door shut when Johnny stopped me, throwing out a quick, "You didn't tell me what the other two reasons you fell for me were."

I paused, nodding as I realized he was right. "I guess I didn't."

"It's okay. You can on our next date."

"No...not dates—"

"Night, Sammy," Johnny said, interrupting me. Then he headed down the hallway whistling, sounding way too smug.

Chapter Five
Sammy

Antonia didn't mind letting us use the empty space she rented out just a few blocks from the center while Johnny got the renovations underway. It wasn't a bad situation, really, since the place had a small kitchen and several bathrooms on the same floor. Johnny had even had his workers bring over our pianos and sound system and set up a small office space for Indra and me to share. The only problem with that was that anything remotely curious that happened caught the attention of my nosy kids, who could see everything we did perfectly through the makeshift walls that separated the classrooms and conference room from the reception area.

Which was why I tried to cut off the flower delivery the second the guy came through the door. It didn't work since the bouquet he carried was large, with at least two dozen white roses and sweet peas, mixed with several other of my favorite flowers.

"Miss Nicola?" the delivery guy asked, holding out the bouquet to me and handing over the vase.

"That's me," I said, tucking the flowers low at my side, hoping the little witnesses to my left wouldn't pay attention. "Thanks," I told the guy, offering him a tip before he hurried back through the door.

"Oh, those are nice," Indra said, taking the bouquet from me before I could chuck them into the garbage. "And there's a card..." She pulled the small white piece of cardstock from the envelope and read what was written. Her expression moved from curious to pleased in under a second. "Well, well, well...looks like you've been holding out on me."

"Have not," I said, ignoring the question in her tone as I moved back to my desk and powered on my laptop. We had a new art class starting that afternoon, and I needed to double-check the instructor's supply list. But Indra was almost as bad as our kids. A fact that was illustrated as she pushed away from her own desk, facing opposite mine, and wheeled her chair back until she landed right next to me.

"You kissed him?" she asked, pinching the card between her fingers.

"Hush," I said, grabbing the card from her before she got truly obnoxious.

Nothing is as sweet as the memory of your kiss.
Thank you for an unforgettable night.
—*JC*

I had to admit it. The man hadn't lost his touch.

"Hey, Miss S, you got a boyfriend now?" I heard, and I turned to see a small group of my kids sticking their heads out of the music lesson. All of them interested in the flowers and the attention I paid to the card that came with them.

"Yes," I told them, standing to pick up the flowers and move them from the spot front and center of the receptionist's desk where Indra had placed them. "Jesus is my boyfriend, and he'll be very upset that you're not practicing your scales. Shoo!"

Laughing, they disappeared, and I forgot about the flowers and Johnny's card for the half second Indra took to turn her chair and lean it back against my mini file cabinet.

"What?" I asked her when she sat there silently, watching me.

"What do you mean, 'What?' I mean, what kind of friend are you anyway? You go on a date with some rich, purportedly hot Italian big shot, and then you get those ridiculous things—" she pointed her thumb over her shoulder toward the flowers "—and you get sent something as sweet as that." She thumped the card in my hand before I dropped it. "I'm going to need details."

If I ignored her, she'd only pout and refuse to do any real work. May as well deal with her right then and there. I inhaled once, swiveling my chair to face her, my hands resting in my lap. The glare I shot at her did nothing to deter her, so I gave up, figuring I'd give her what she wanted and be done with this conversation.

"What would you like to know?"

Indra sat up, and if I didn't know her better, I'd say she was tempted to clap or do a little happy dance. But she composed herself enough to sit on one foot, getting comfortable before she faced me. "He kissed you?" I nodded, pulling Indra's smile wide. "Tongue or no tongue?"

I exhaled and rolled my eyes, feeling a tension headache already building. "Tiny bit of tongue, but nothing pornographic."

She copied my eye roll. "You could use pornographic, if you want my opinion."

"I don't. Anything else?"

"*Duh.* Details." She moved her chair closer, glancing once over her shoulder toward the wall of glass that separated the lobby area and the rehearsing student musicians before she returned her attention to me. "So, did he just go up to you and kiss you, or was it smooth? Did he have moves? Tell me how it happened."

A quick flash of that kiss rushed into my mind, and I suppressed the memory. It was a good kiss. Too good, but I couldn't let myself get caught up in what

I knew was an impossible situation. Johnny wasn't a good man. He never would be. It didn't matter how good of a kisser he was. Or that he was even better at it as a man than he had been as an eighteen-year-old kid.

Nothing would ever happen between us.

But I couldn't tell Indra that. She stared at me. Her hopeful, romantic-comedy, Hallmark-movie-loving, doe eyes watching me like she fully expected me to tell her something fit for a goofy Christmas romance movie. I couldn't disappoint her, but I wouldn't lie either.

"It was a great kiss. But it was all pretend. The Garcias asked how we met, Johnny told the truth and then lied by saying I was giving him a second chance."

"I'm not sure that's a lie, Sam."

"Anyway," I said, ignoring the stupid grin on her face and her assumption. "They insisted he kiss me. End of story."

"Well, that's disappointing." When I didn't argue, Indra's attention returned to me. "What's that look? You were disappointed?"

"Not exactly." Even I couldn't recover that quickly. Indra knew me well. She could make out when I was trying to hide what I thought or when something disappointed me. Even if I knew nothing could happen between Johnny and me, it didn't mean I wasn't sorry the kiss had ended so quickly.

"It's not that... Later on, he tried to make me believe he actually had plans for winning me back." Indra smiled, and I almost hated to disappoint her with the shake of my head. "Sorry, no. Not going to happen. Besides, I messed that up pretty badly. I told him he had no honor, and for someone like Johnny Carelli, that's below the belt."

"But not untrue."

I let loose a low laugh, but it held no humor. She couldn't know how accurate her words were, and I had no intention of ever telling her. Indra knew enough about me. But not everything. "No, not entirely."

"So, did you apologize?" I nodded, and Indra seemed satisfied.

"And then he tried to convince me I'd let him date me."

She relaxed against her chair, her smile easy, satisfied as she moved her fingers over her mouth as though she were thinking about something that pleased her greatly. After a few seconds, Indra nodded. "He's got balls. I think I might love him. You need someone like that."

"I've been there with him before," I told her, turning my chair to focus on my laptop again. "It didn't end well."

"But still. You were attracted once." She ignored my body language and the way I tried to appear busy by scanning through my unopened emails. Indra moved her chair next to me, still talking, seeming not to care that I was ready for this conversation to end. "And it stuck with you if you're still a little sweet on him."

"I'm not."

I hated her laugh, how quick it came, how it made me feel like an idiot.

It only quieted when I jerked my gaze to her, my features going tight. "He broke me."

Indra went quiet. I hadn't meant to make her feel bad, but by how silent she'd become, my confession had made her understand that I wasn't ready to give Johnny Carelli any second chances.

After a minute, she touched my hand, squeezing it once, only relaxing again when I returned her smile.

"It's fine. It's really not that big of a deal."

"You say that," Indra started, her voice cautious, "but I've never seen you get so uneasy about a guy. Men throw themselves at you all the time. Gorgeous men. Powerful men. Well-connected men. And you brush them off like they're nothing. This one, though. This one rattles you, and inside a few weeks of reconnecting with him, you've agreed to an arrangement with him and let him kiss you. I guess I just have to wonder why. What is it about him?" Indra tilted her head, her focus sharp as she looked me over. "Are you really over him?"

He had soft, wet lips and held me so close. His breath was warm, smelled like mint and wine. I thought he might devour me. I thought maybe I wanted him to. Just for a second, only for a second, I thought I wanted him to ravish me like he had before.

Before...before he destroyed me and left me with...

I blinked, squashing the heartache, trying to remember what came next. The sweetness. The joy. There was so much of it that had nothing to do with Johnny. So much more to come. I'd stopped hating him a long time ago, and it was because of who I became after he left me behind.

He changed me, and part of me loved him for that.

But that didn't mean I could ever let myself be in love with him again.

I forced a small smile, dismissing Indra's laugh as I went back to my email, clicking through one message after another. "Of course I'm over him," I told my friend as I set about my work.

Four hours later, Indra had gone to fetch our lunch. The kids were still in the middle of their impromptu picnics in the rehearsal space, ditching their instruments in favor of singing a cappella rounds of mash-up songs most of the clergy they performed for likely wouldn't approve of.

I tidied the office space, ignoring the flowers Indra had returned back to the receptionist's desk even after my second and third attempts to chuck them. Despite the small irksome feeling I had for Johnny for sending me such an obviously expensive gift, I couldn't help but appreciate the bouquet. They were beautiful, and their scent filled the entire lobby area. The petals were soft, delicate, and I touched one, rubbing the rose in what could only be described as a lapse of good sense, just as the front door opened and a deep voice said to my right, "Good. I'm glad you got them."

Of course, he'd show right then.

I jerked around, lifting my chin to face him like a soldier readying for battle. Why did I always feel like I had to be on my guard with this man?

Ah. That's right. Because he'd conquered me once already.

"Johnny," I greeted, not bothering to acknowledge the flowers at all. "What are you doing here?"

His gaze shifted to the bouquet, then back to me. I spotted the small twitch moving his thick lips. It surprised me that whatever sarcastic comment I was convinced he wanted to make stayed clamped down behind his mouth. "Ah, there is a designer I'd like you to meet. He's down the block at another appointment and could squeeze you in this afternoon if you have time."

"You couldn't call?" I asked, not convinced that was the real reason he'd stopped in. Folding my arms, I waited for him to answer me. I was surprised when he looked away, scanning the room, caught sight of the kids, and stepped away to look down the hallway to the back of the area. "Johnny?"

"Sorry, *bella,*" he said, returning to me. "I confess, I wanted to see how everything looked and make sure you got settled in okay."

I wasn't buying it. "No, you wanted to make sure your little cousin did everything she promised she'd do."

Johnny furrowed his eyebrows, and a deep line formed between them. But as I went on staring at him, not removing the knowing frown from my lips, he relented, laughing. "Fine. That too. But, *oddio,* she's charging me through the nose. I want to make sure she's giving me what I'm paying for."

"Do you want a tour?" I offered, waving a hand toward the hallway.

He frowned before he looked down at his watch. "No, but thank you. I don't want to disrupt your day any more than I have. But I did mean what I said about Rico coming by. Is this afternoon okay? Maybe around four?"

"We don't need a designer, Johnny. That's not what the center is about," I told him, pulling my arms around my waist when he stepped closer to me.

"He's not *that* kind of designer, *bella*. His focus is on developmental education and urban community centers. You think I'd send some bougie asshole into your center to make it look ridiculous?" He glanced toward the kids when the a cappella singing grew louder. They'd begun to add claps and a few foot stomps to provide more rhythm. "I want your kids to feel comfortable." He faced me again, a small smile stretching his mouth. "And I want you to be happy."

Damn you, Johnny Carelli.

Why did he have to say things like that? I dropped my arms but balled my fists, trying to keep from reaching up and hugging him. It would send the wrong message to my kids...and to him, but saints preserve me, that was the nicest thing he'd ever said to me.

"Johnny..." I tried, a little embarrassed when my words came out clogged and thick.

"Bella," he interrupted and took my hand. "I'd do anything for you. Anything at all."

I could only stare up at him. My mind went blank of anything but the glint in his eyes and how dark the pupils were. My God, he was beautiful and his mouth looked so soft, so inviting. He was a scoundrel, and he drove home that point by choosing that exact moment to tuck the center of his fat bottom lip between his teeth. Something I'd seen him do a thousand times as a kid. Something that never failed to elicit an automatic primal reaction from my body.

I swallowed, pulling my gaze upward, and without really knowing why I did it, I took a step toward him. Like I was drawn by something I couldn't name, wanting him with a fierceness I hadn't felt in ten long, *long* years.

"I...want..." It was all I could manage before I remembered where and who I was. Then I stepped back, blinking, bumping into the receptionist's desk in my hurry to put space between us. The action was so fast that the bouquet of flowers began to topple, and Johnny lunged for it, shooting out one of his long arms to catch it.

He held himself close, with one hand on the vase of flowers, the other near my arm on the desk. "Got 'em," he said, looking at me, his breath heavy and warm over my forehead as he spoke. God, he smelled good. So good, in fact, that I had to close my eyes, helpless to do anything but inhale that rich, decadent scent of his expensive cologne. "You good, *bella?*"

"Yes," I answered, opening my eyes when I felt the soft touch of Johnny's thumb smoothing down my cheek. "What are you..." I frowned, straightening where I stood.

"Sorry." He stepped back. He didn't put much space between us, but it was enough that his scent didn't make me feel drunk. "You know," he started, the humor back in his voice, "you never told me what the second thing was."

It took me a moment to understand his meaning, but the memory of the last time we saw each other came back to me and so did my hurried explanation of why I'd fallen for him to make an excuse for saying he had no honor.

"I didn't."

Johnny's smile was wider now and more relaxed, as though he was happy I was playing along with him.

"And I'm pretty sure I never promised I would."

76

He jutted his chin, motioning to the flowers. "Those were pretty expensive, and I did rescue them. Humor me. What was the second thing?"

He laughed when I shook my head. "You are in need of constant affirmation, aren't you?"

"What can I say? I'm a needy guy."

"Oh, that is without a doubt." Again, I crossed my arms, pretending I was more annoyed with his question than with him before I released an exaggerated breath. "Fine, if you must know. It was…your eyes."

Johnny squinted, as though he didn't trust my answer, head cocking to the side. "My eyes?"

"That's what I said."

"My dark, boring eyes? Dario says I have shit-brown eyes."

Helpless to hold back, I laughed, remembering Johnny's cousin and how often the kid I knew would say and do whatever struck him. He never gave much thought to anything at all. No wonder he'd landed in prison.

"No," I told Johnny, remembering all those stolen nights away from my uncle, away from both our families and the lives and responsibilities forced on us. "Dark and fathomless. Endless. I remember wanting to stare forever into those dark eyes to see just how lost I could get in them."He watched me for a few seconds, mouth opening and closing like he wasn't quite sure what he wanted to say or how to get the words out. Finally, he inhaled and spoke on a soft, exhale of, "Why, *bella?*" His voice was gentle, tone a little breathless.

"Because, Johnny." I looked him in the eyes, lost now in the memory, in the same color, the same depth that had never failed to intoxicate me. For a second, I forgot where I was or why I was admitting anything to him. "I thought maybe if I got lost and you got lost, we'd find a way to anchor each other."

The second the admission came, I realized I'd said too much.

It was too honest.

Too real for the moment.

The heartache was always there, waiting for one of us to uncover it.

I'd managed a decade with it buried in a shallow grave. It was always just below the surface. From the expression on his face, I got the impression that wound had been exorcised, buried so deep, only God could resurrect it. And with one small admission, I'd done what only the Almighty could.

"Bella," he started but stopped when I looked away from him.

Too much. Too real and we both knew it.

"Well," he tried again, clearing his throat. He pulled my attention back to him by grabbing my hand, forcing me to look up. I was sure he'd kiss my knuckles. He had the night after our dinner with the Garcias. But it seemed Johnny was upping his game. He was sweetening the pot. "I hope you enjoy the flowers, Sammy. They aren't nearly as beautiful as you." Then he leaned forward, touching his lips to my cheek. Maybe he would have stayed there, just kissing my cheek, pressing his chest to mine, his palm to my back, moving us together like it was the most natural, necessary position for our bodies to be in. Maybe he would have gone in for another kiss, making a play for my lips. But just as I looked up, a loud roar of laughter sounded at our side, and my kids released a resounding squeal of noise that sounded like a perfectly pitched chorus of "Woo-hoo!"

Johnny stepped back, laughing at their catcalls and a few refrains of "Oh, Miss S!" and one even louder, "He don't look like Jesus!" before they were pushed back into the conference room.

"You should go," I told him, my face flushing hot as the kids went on hooting at us through the glass wall.

"Yeah," Johnny said, pointing at a few of the boys. "I think I will." But before he left, the man took my hand and kissed it, squeezing my fingers before he turned to leave. His steps were swift but calm. His stride was easy, but his back was stiff, his shoulders tight, and I felt somehow guilty for making him look so on edge.

He was almost to the door before he stopped, glancing at me one last time. "You know, Sammy, you weren't the only one who found an anchor."

And then he was gone, leaving me with nothing but the hooting and hollering of those teasing, giddy kids and the memory of something I wasn't sure could ever be repaired.

Chapter Six
Johnny

Sofia, my sister Cara's high school friend, ran Così Buono like it was her home kitchen and not a five-star restaurant. The food was the best in the city, the wine was the richest, and there was always a private table waiting for our family anytime we wanted to celebrate. Tonight, we had a reason.

Dario was home.

I sat with Cara and her husband, Kiel, along with our cousins, around a large table at the front of the place, drinking too much wine. Smoke, or Dimitri, as my aunt and uncle named him, and Dario argued with their sister Antonia about which of them had been the first to successfully sneak out of their father's palatial mansion without any of his guards or their perceptive mother ever finding out.

"It wasn't you, *mimma*," Dario told his little sister, his voice low with gravel in it that hadn't been there five years before when he'd been sent to Rikers. Doing time had worn him down a bit, but now Dario was back. And, God willing, being back and staying out would take the edge from him.

This dinner, Smoke had told us, might be the start of it. He wanted things to be normal for Dario.

Guess that meant making him feel as though he hadn't spent a day away from them.

Antonia was doing her best with that. "You *chooch*, it *was* me," she told her brother, the frown showing everyone around the table that she was offended by his statement. But she said it with a laugh in her tone, something she always did. "I've got the scar on my leg to prove it!"

My little cousin was beautiful, like all Carelli women, and no one ever really took her seriously—until they were across a desk from her, negotiating a contract. Something I found out a few weeks back when I tried to sweet-talk my way into a lower rent for the space Sammy needed while her center was being renovated. Antonia had turned me down flat. "I love Sammy, but friends or not, family or not," she'd informed me, "business is business. Pay me what I ask, or I'll rent the space to someone else."

"Toni, I'm telling you," Dario tried, leaning on his elbows as his sister glared at him. "You think Papa didn't know? Or Micky and Nick? They told Papa the second you and Cara here hit the city." He nodded to my sister, winking at her when her mouth dropped open. "Papa had Micky and his boys following you two that whole weekend." He nodded at the waitress when she poured him another glass of wine and immediately drank half the contents. He glanced at Smoke, looking to his older brother to confirm the truth. When the man nodded, not seeming the least bit sorry to disappoint his kid sister, Antonia slapped her hand to the table, making a noise that sounded like a laugh and a scream all at once.

"Son of a bitch!" she said, bouncing back against her chair, ignoring the laughs she got as she and Cara leaned across Kiel, mumbling about whatever shit they'd done that they were only now discovering their fathers had long known about.

"Yeah," Dario said, not bothering to stifle his laugh. "They knew about the boys from Long Island with the ten-inch—""That's enough," Cara interrupted when Kiel leaned forward, trying to hear what Dario was saying, despite Antonia tossing her napkin at him to keep him quiet.

"It was a long time ago," I explained to my brother-in-law, who only grinned, taking the kiss my sister gave him as she excused herself from the table to run to the bathroom. Antonia sulked with her own glass of red, shooting mock glares at her brother, who kept a grin on his face.

"This is good," Smoke said to me, a whiskey tumbler hanging loosely from his fingers. Of all of my uncle's kids, Smoke was the smartest and, I had to admit, the coolest. Uncle Sonny was younger than my father, and he'd never been interested in the level of involvement in the family business that Papa ran. He preferred a simpler life, running more legitimate businesses. Though, there were elements in his dealings that did require things that most folks might frown upon. Smoke handled the bulk of those dealings now that Uncle Sonny was retired, and since Dario was out, he'd probably give Smoke a hand.

"The fighting?" I asked Smoke, spotting Cara talking to Sofia at the hostess desk through the glass doors separating our private dining room from the rest of the restaurant.

"All of us being together," he said, his gaze shooting to his two younger siblings as Antonia moved between Dario and Kiel to share my brother-in-law's phone. I heard "Keleu" and knew they were looking at pictures of my baby nephew. "It's been a long time since we were all together."

"When will Dante be back?" I asked, wondering if the youngest of Uncle Sonny's kids would even be welcome back in Bronxville. He'd been an idiot, trying to run drugs out of Dario's legitimate bar. But Dante was a spoiled kid, always had been. Instead of making him do the bid, Dario took the blame, serving the time that belonged to his kid brother.

"Hmmm," Smoke said, swirling the whiskey in his glass before he downed it. He barely got the tumbler back onto the table before the pretty blond waitress replaced it, shooting an eager smile to my younger cousin as she walked away. He appreciated the way she did that, but then he answered me. "Papa's caved to Mama. Dante lands next week from Pistoia after five years working at our uncle Anthony's vineyard."

"Think it helped?" I asked, calling off the waitress when she asked to top off my nearly full glass.

"I think five years in the hot Tuscan sun fertilizing soil, pruning vines, and picking grapes for virtually no money at all, eighteen hours a day, under the supervision of a man who doesn't believe any man under the age of twenty-five should be doing anything but learning how to work a vineyard, is bound to teach humility." Smoke took another swig of his whiskey then shrugged, glancing at his brother and sister as they watched a video on Kiel's phone of the baby. "If it doesn't, then there's no hope for that asshole."

"We all do stupid shit when we're kids, man." God knew I had. Sometimes I thought there'd be no making up for the destruction I'd left behind when I lied to Sammy. As I watched Sofia and my sister through the doors, I thought maybe I didn't deserve forgiveness.

"There's a big difference between fucking an off-limits girl," Smoke said, and I jerked my attention back to him, "and fucking over your blood."

I had no idea how he knew about Sammy and me. I thought Cara had been the only one who knew anything about us, but Smoke was smooth on his worst days. Hell, he got the name Smoke by boxing in college, because in under two rounds, that's exactly what he'd do to his opponents—smoke them. Later, when he went to work for his father, he earned a reputation for picking up info that gave him an upper hand. He was a guy who knew shit, and that shit led to him smoking the competition. Besides, if memory served, Smoke spent an entire summer his senior year of college in the city interning for some Wall Street big shot. He'd dated Sofia back then, and Sofia was Cara's best friend. Like an idiot, I'd told Cara about Sammy and me. Two and two almost always made four in our family.

"Maybe you're right," I told my cousin, hoping, for Dante's sake, that he'd actually learned his lesson. His parents may be forgiving, maybe even his sister and brother Dario were, but by the way just mentioning the kid had made Smoke's jaw clench and his grip tighten on his tumbler, I got the feeling his forgiveness would be harder to earn.

Smoke shrugged, dismissing the topic by taking another drink, but then his attention caught across the room. And I followed his gaze, narrowing my eyes when I spotted Liam Shane standing a little too close to Sofia and Cara at the hostess stand. That asshole was always sniffing around women who hadn't invited his attention. It had gotten him in hot water with his uncle Ian, head of the McKinney family, but that hadn't stopped him from making messes for his uncle to clean up. He'd already knocked up a young girl back in Ireland and was rumored to have a wife somewhere that no one could find.

Next to me, Dario shot the man a glare, and I got the feeling there was something more to that look than just Shane standing too close to Cara. My cousin curled his fist, looked ready to jump from his spot, but Smoke cleared his throat, catching Dario's attention, and he grabbed his wine, downing what was left of it in one swig.

I made to stand, ready to have a word with the bastard about leaving, but it seemed my brother-in-law was quicker. Kiel shot out of his chair, a quick smile on his face, and made it to his wife and her friend, forcing his hand out to Shane for a shake. When the guy took too long to take it, Kiel clapped him on the shoulder, escorting him out of the restaurant with two of Sofia's beefier dishwashers following behind him.

"I like this husband of Cara's," Smoke said, and I glanced at my cousin, grinning.

"*Si.* He'll do."

My cousin's smirk widened, and he moved his head again, motioning back toward the front of the restaurant. "Your night just got better," he said, eyebrows arching up like he thought I should pay attention.

I turned, spotting Cara walking back in, pulling on Sammy's hand as she reluctantly trailed behind her while Kiel ushered both women into the private dining room. I didn't even think about what I was doing. I stood, jabbing Dario in the shoulder, ignoring my cousin when he looked up at me. "Move over, *si?*" I said, walking over to greet Sammy. *"Bella."* She didn't flinch when I leaned down to kiss her cheek or argue when I led her toward the table, right to the seat Dario had vacated.

"Samantha Nicola," my cousin said, his deep, gravelly tone lifting almost an octave as he watched her sit down, her cheeks turning pink. She never liked being the center of attention.

"Dario, it's good to see you." She turned toward him, kissing his cheeks like they were old friends, and the tease in my cousin's tone vanished. She greeted him like she always had when we were kids, not like some felon who'd been locked up in one of the roughest penitentiaries in the country. He seemed to appreciate that. "I told Cara I didn't want to interrupt..."

"And I told you," Cara said, "you aren't interrupting. We're all friends and family here." She called over a waitress and pointed to Sammy. "Can you grab the order she placed in the kitchen and bring it to the table? She'll eat with us. Oh, and bring her a glass. She drinks red too."

"Well, I really don't..."

"You know how stubborn Cara is, *bella,*" I told Sammy, leaning toward her to be heard over the loud conversation that had started back up when Antonia challenged Smoke about how often he got caught sneaking girls into his room.

To which, the man told his little sister, "I've never been *caught* doing anything."

"Just like her brother," Sammy said, finally turning her head to look at me. There was a slow, sweet grin on her lips as she moved her gaze over my face.

I wanted to kiss her right then, almost more than I had two days ago when I'd stopped by to tell her about the designer meeting with her. She'd been honest with me, real. It had been the first time I'd seen that, really seen that from her since we were kids, and I'd been aching for more of the same.

There was so much noise around us—my family being loud and obnoxious, the waitstaff buzzing around us to make sure the bread and drinks had been replenished. But the only thing I noticed was that faint rosemary scent coming off Sammy's long, thick hair and how the dim light above us reflected in her bright green eyes.

Sammy watched me with her elbows resting on the table, her chin on her knuckles and the gorgeous, movie-star face turned toward me like a work of art etched out of marble. So much flawless perfection and only I was allowed to see her this way.

"What are you looking at, Johnny Carelli?" she asked.

She was so close and not close enough at all.

"Everything, Sammy. Absolutely everything."

Sammy hadn't smiled at me this much since the night of her eighteenth birthday. But I think that was mainly because her uncle had allowed her to leave with Cara, thinking she'd stay all night with my sister in the pool house of my father's home, watching movies and swimming under the careful supervision of his guards. Cara had acted like a good friend, which she had been at the time. But she'd been a better sister, convincing our father that she and Sammy were tired and would spend the night alone in the pool house. Sammy did, at least. Cara didn't. My sister slipped out at eleven, hours after my father went to sleep, and I met Sammy to give her my present—me.

It had been the best night of my life. Touching her, tasting her, feeling everywhere I'd only teased, every sweet part I'd dreamed about but wasn't allowed. She'd been relaxed, calm afterward, falling into me, wanting me again and again, teasing me herself, making jokes until we were both breathless.

Tonight, I'd seen a bit of that girl, surrounded by my family, watching Antonia being teased by her brothers, hearing Kiel giving back all that we gave him. Sammy laughed at us, all of us, and my God had she been beautiful doing it.

"It's good that Dario is home," she said, walking next to me as I led her down the hallway to her door. "I haven't seen Antonia that happy in a long time."

"Me either."

My cousins ended the night by closing the restaurant, waving me, Sammy, Kiel, and Cara away as we made our goodnights. Last glance I took, I spotted the three of them huddled at the end of the table sharing a bottle of bourbon, heads together as they talked. Smoke was right. It had been good to see. I worried about Dario, about how he'd do after so long locked inside. Some people weren't ever the same again, but he wasn't just some people. He was a Carelli. Besides, family never leaves you, no matter how many hurdles you throw in its way.

"You think he'll be okay?" Sammy asked, seeming to read my mind. She tilted her head, looking curious when I moved my eyebrows up. "What?"

"I was just wondering that myself."

She leaned back against the wall next to her door, her keys dangling from her finger. "Is this where you tell me we've always had this stupid psychic connection?""Think that would get me inside?"

She laughed, likely a little buzzed or, at least, relaxed enough not to be bothered when I moved a palm next to her head on the wall and stared down at her. "No. It won't," Sammy said. She looked like she wanted to argue with me, may have even been thinking of something clever and sarcastic to say, but I moved then, lifting her chin with my knuckle. And the smile and smartass comment disappeared from her mouth. "What...what are you doing?" Her question came out in a long, panting breath, but Sammy knew what I wanted. It was the same thing she'd wanted from me since the day I sent her the flowers.

"Can't you figure it out?"

She'd always been a good girl, sweet, dutiful. But when I had her, she opened up, became passionate, primal. I saw hints of the woman she was, the creature she had been, surfacing as I moved closer toward her.

"Sammy, you tell me to walk away, and I will." I inhaled, my mouth watering at the hint of wine I smelled on her breath and the heat coming from her body. "But I want you to know, because I don't think I'm the only one thinking these things here...that I want you. I want to taste every inch of you." I moved closer still, turning her face to press the slightest hint of a kiss against the shell of her ear. "From your ear," I said, sucking on the lobe, loving how she shook against me, "to the long, sweet slope of your neck." I kissed her there, running my wet mouth along her neck, down to her clavicle, and Sammy curled her arms around my shoulders, trembling now as though she needed to anchor herself to something solid and steady. She went on shaking, her body going limp when I pressed against her, holding her by the waist to push her into me. "Tell me now," I said next to her ear. "I'm a patient man. I can wait for you. You want me to leave, I will. I'll go home and think about how many ways I want to take you and taste you." At that, the grip she had on my shoulders tightened, and Sammy slipped her fingers into my hair. "If you don't, I'm going to rush you into your apartment. I'm going to take off that pretty little skirt of yours and slip your panties down those long, beautiful legs." A low, whining groan left her throat, and her grip on my hair tightened. "Then I'm going to lean you back on whatever flat surface I find and spread you wide. I'm going to make you wet, *bella,* and I'm going to fucking devour you."

"Johnny...ah..."

There was a hesitation. It would always be there. I'd hurt her so much. She was doubting the wisdom of us together. Maybe she always would. But she knew, I think, somewhere deep down inside her, she knew I really was sorry. "*Bella,*" I tried, my voice serious, my gaze on hers. "I'm not the kid who broke your heart anymore." I kissed her mouth one slow, sweet time. "I'll never be him again."

She watched me then, a decision seeming to work through her eyes, her expression shifting from hesitation to fear then back to lust when I licked my bottom lip again.

"Tell me," I said, pulling back to see her expression. "Do you want me to walk away or take you inside?"

She sucked on her lip, her body pressed tightly to mine, hands shifting until her palms were flat on my cheeks. And Samantha Nicola, the most beautiful woman I'd ever known, kissed me right on the mouth. It took me a second to realize what she was doing. It took three more to wonder if this was a goodbye or an invitation into her home, but then as soon as the kiss started, just before I'd fully started to enjoy it, Sammy backed away, staring up at me with her eyes all dark and wide, her mouth plump and wet from our kiss.

"Take me inside, Johnny. Right now."

Chapter Seven

Sammy

He took control. Always. Two sentences and Johnny opened my door, throwing my keys and bag to the floor. He had me in his arms, and I didn't care. He kissed me like he owned me and, in that moment, I guess he did. I allowed myself to admit he always had.

I didn't think about anything but the way he moved over me, how his mouth demanded, how there was so much strength in his hands, how he unbuttoned my shirt and slipped my zipper, then my skirt, down my legs. And then I found myself standing there, in the center of my living room with only the table lamp to light the entire apartment, in just my underwear and heels, with Johnny Carelli watching me, sizing me up like I was the prey and he was a starving lion.

I wasn't a teenager anymore. Nearing thirty put miles on my body, but I wasn't ashamed or embarrassed. If he expected me to look like I had ten years ago, he'd be disappointed. But then, Johnny only seemed concerned with looking me over, with tearing his jacket off and prowling forward, grabbing me by the hips, and holding me against his body again. He was so hard all over—his arms, his chest, his stomach, his...my goodness, everywhere I could imagine.

"Sammy, go to the couch," he demanded, nodded like he knew I'd only have to be told once. I didn't like being bossed around, but something deep inside me liked the expression on Johnny's face when I walked away from him. It seemed to make him happy to watch me move.

"You like seeing that?" I asked, walking backward, smile widening when he nodded, not speaking a word. "Do you like it more when I do this?" I turned, wondering where I'd summoned the bravado to show him my naked backside, fully aware I'd worn a thong that morning. The groan of pleasure he released was satisfaction enough to tamp down any ego-smashing I might have felt at him telling me what to do.

"*Oddio, bella,* that ass..."

"You like it?" I knew he did, especially when he hurried toward me, untucking his button-up shirt and kicking off his shoes. He reached for his pants, but he stopped short when I slipped my fingers underneath the thin straps at my hips, tugging at them. The hungry smile on his face lowered, replaced by something that looked ancient and primitive, something I'd only seen from Johnny once, a very long time ago.

"I like everything you do, Samantha." He stood in front of me and reached for my wrists, taking both in his hands to pepper kisses along the insides of my arms and loop them around his neck. Johnny seemed to love my fingers in his hair, and he moved them there as he went to his knees, kissing between my breasts, holding my back to tease my ribs, then my stomach with slow, wet kisses as the hold I had on his hair went tighter. "Delicious," he mumbled against my skin, slowing his attentions when he took hold of my thong, moving the straps down, his gaze up at my face, watching me, looking closely as he slipped the fabric down my legs.

Another kiss landed on one hip, followed by a second, then Johnny looked at me again, teasing the insides of my thighs with the tips of his fingers. My stomach jumped, and the tightness working deep inside me quickened until I felt wetter, until the heat he stirred inside me had my nipples hardening.

"Touch me," I said, pulling him close as my eyes slid closed.

Johnny obeyed, groaning as he fingered me slowly.

"Johnny..."

"Sit down, *bella*. I wanna taste you."

Seconds after he led me to the couch and moved between my knees, holding me open to him, his hands flat against my thighs, his palms spreading me apart, Johnny kissed my center. He licked me at first with long swipes of his tongue, devouring me like a meal just as he promised. Then as the sensation began to build and I pressed his head closer and closer, Johnny slipped two fingers inside me, seeming to hold me everywhere—at my core, at the legs, in my mind, even at my breasts when he reached up with his free hand to pull down my bra and tease my hardened nipple.

"Johnny... Oh God... I'm so close..."

Every inch of me felt electrified. And it was him, the sensation of Johnny—the boy I'd loved, the man I wanted and should never, ever be with—tasting me, waking up all the long-dead sensations I'd told myself I'd never feel again. No one had ever touched me like this. No one had ever made my body sing and soar quite like he did.

"*Bella*...I feel how tight you are..." he said, still fingering me, head lifting to watch me as he found that spot deep inside me and teased it into oblivion. "So wet and tight and fucking perfect." Johnny moved forward, licking my nipple, sucking hard, nibbling it as he continued to work me from the inside. I clenched around him, wanting that pending climax to reach me. "*Cuore mio,* you are beautiful and so delicious." He moved his hands faster, worked hard as he took my mouth. "Come for me, love. I want to see you."

Several seconds later, with Johnny moving his hand, working my sweet spot, and his attention back on my nipple, I finally came. But when I did, everything brightened and lifted, the world around me like a carnival of sensation I never wanted to leave. Ripples of bliss and pleasure washed over me until I couldn't breathe. Until the only thing I could register was Johnny's warm, soft kisses against my neck and the sweet, throbbing sensation between my legs. I was sated but not finished.

He lay next to me, smiling, his hands resting on my backside. He kissed over my shoulder as he lowered the strap of my bra until he finally moved me, shifting our positions. I straddled him on my couch, liking the power I felt looming over him. The expression of sheer eager desire on Johnny's face as he lowered my bra and stared openly at my naked body.

We didn't speak as he touched me. The slow trek of his fingertips across my collarbone, between my breasts, followed by the shift of his gaze, said enough to me. He was ready to burst from wanting me, and I felt the same.

Johnny seemed to hold his breath as I leaned forward. The tips of my nipples touched each expanse of skin exposed when I unbuttoned his shirt and pushed apart the fabric. He was still so beautiful.

"What's this?" I asked, touching a long, white scar that ran down the center of his chest. It was the only imperfection on his solid, muscular chest.

"I was reckless for a long time," he admitted, brushing the hair off my forehead when I leaned forward to get a better look at the scar. "It was a long time ago."

I kissed it anyway, loving the smile he gave me and the low, growling noise of pleasure he released when that simple kiss transformed. I inched down his body, to his flat, taut abdomen. I watched him, a little empowered when Johnny bit his lip as I unbuckled his belt and unfastened his pants, releasing the zipper until I gripped him in my hands.

"Fuck, Sammy...*oddio*..."

He was beautiful, from the strength of his large, muscular frame to the perfect contours of his big dick. I held it. Loving the weight of it. Loving the power I felt just taking it in my hand. I closed my mouth over the head, licking the tip, remembering this and how much he'd enjoyed when I tasted him here.

Immediately, Johnny began a rushed, muted litany of words I couldn't make out, incomprehensible things he said to himself that I took as complimentary. But when I stroked him, still holding him in my mouth, Johnny stiffened. He gripped my arms, flipping us, until I was on my back and he lay on top of me.

He rose up on his elbows, using his knee to move my legs apart as he held himself above, ready to enter me. "For the love of Christ, tell me you're on something."

"The shot." I smiled, looking up, waiting. "And you?"

"I can't get pregnant, *bella*." When I frowned, he laughed, scrubbing his face. "Clean. On my parents' graves, I'm clean." The smallest nod from me and Johnny moved forward, kissing me. His mouth pressed hard, tongue demanding as he put his weight onto both palms and slipped into me. When he was fully inside and thrust his hips once, we both exhaled, breathing out a strangled pant as ten long years of loss, of distance, of so many lies and deceit shifted, and there was only the two of us pushed back together, settled into this moment.

"*Ah*...Johnny," I said, lifting my legs, loving that he held one in his hand as he surged forward.

"Sammy, God, baby...I've missed you."

We would have gone on like that, maybe spent the entire night wrapped up in each other, enjoying each other's bodies, making up for the time we'd lost. But as Johnny started to make love to me and his movements began to quicken, my cell phone rang, interrupting the fog of pleasure.

"Get up," I said, not caring that he tried to argue.

"Sammy..."

"Johnny, get off me."

"Let your voice mail..."

"No, I can't." He moved, likely hearing the panic I knew was in my voice. I wiggled away from him and darted around the room, grabbing my purse from the floor to dig for my phone. I managed to answer before the caller hung up.

"Hello?" I said, seeing Johnny in my peripheral as he sat on the couch. He didn't bother to cover that beautiful body as he watched me. The voice on the other end was professional, giving me a name I didn't know from the hospital more than an hour away. "Yes," I answered when asked if I was who I was supposed to be. "That's me." Then came the news I'd dreaded for ten years. The news everyone in my position always dreaded and went on dreading until they were in the ground. "Of course. Yes. I'll be there as soon as possible. Thank you."

I closed my eyes, breathing in and out, only then realizing the firestorm of drama I'd be in if Johnny asked for details. Who was I kidding? Of course, he was going to ask. Despite what had just happened between us, I couldn't let him know. Not like this.

"Everything okay?" he asked, standing when I began to search around the living room for my clothes.

"I...uh..." I shook my head, trying to calm myself, trying to remember my priorities and to put on my game face. Johnny was *here*. He was right here. My God, this was incredibly stupid, letting him inside my home. If we hadn't been consumed with lust, if we'd had sex and he'd stayed the night, he'd have woken up in the morning and spotted pictures and items, and he would have had a thousand questions. What the hell was I thinking? Ah. That's right. I hadn't been thinking much at all.

"Not really, no," I said, slipping on my skirt and tugging on my shirt. "I...uh...I'm the next of kin for a friend of mine. That was the Ellenville Hospital. They've been brought in, and I've got to go."

"Ellenville?" He blinked at me, recovering quickly when I didn't elaborate, and then shrugged. "I'll take you," he said, like it was a statement, not an offer.

"No." I stopped him when he opened his mouth to argue.

"Sammy, that's a two-hour car ride."

"I'm aware, Johnny. I've driven it before. I don't need a ride." Johnny looked to the disarray of clothes, to the pillows and cushions disrupted by what we'd been doing and then shook his head as though he couldn't believe I was dismissing him so easily. "Please," I told him, hoping that my tone made him understand. "This is...personal. I can't have you there."

"I'm not..." He swung his hand around the room. "This wasn't personal?"

"Different kind of personal, Johnny."

He wouldn't understand. In fact, if he knew the truth, he'd hate me. For just a moment longer, I wanted to keep that from happening. Johnny's frown relaxed to worry when I stepped in front of him, pulling his face between my hands to kiss him. "I've been me for a long time. I haven't needed anyone's help. You can't expect that to change overnight. My business is my business, even when it comes to you."

He watched me then, but I knew he wasn't satisfied. After several moments, he nodded, kissing me before he got dressed. He accompanied me downstairs to my car.

"If you need me..."

"You'll be the first person I call," I lied, hopping in my car when the attendant brought it around from the garage. As I pulled away, I watched Johnny in the rearview, praying he'd get in his car and go home. Hoping like hell he'd let me keep this secret a little while longer.

The hospital was beige and sterile, like most were, but the children's ward, at least, had waves of pink, blue, and green balloons painted along the walls leading to the various wings. It was a green wave that led to the nurses station in the ER when I arrived. My hands were still shaking from the trip and the repeated messages sent to me by the camp director.

She's fine, Ms. Nicola. I promise. Just a touch of food poisoning, but she was asking for you.

The woman had only been camp director for a year. She didn't know Betta. So how in the world would she know if the girl was fine or not?

The nurse in the blue scrubs scribbled something on a chart while sipping on a bottle of water. She had red hair and a riot of freckles, and when she spotted me, flashed a crooked smile. "Oh, you gotta belong to green eyes in curtain four, right?"

"Elizabetta Nicola?"

"Poor thing. It was trout, I think they said. Dang," she continued, giving me a once-over. "I've seen family resemblances, but my God..."

"Where is she?"

"Just down there. Curtain four..."

I followed the direction she indicated with her blue-inked Bic and hurried to the green curtain and the label of FOUR, peeking my head around it to find the tiny form lying on her side, with a scratchy-looking wool blanket covering her long legs.

She didn't move when I sat on the bed next to her and immediately started my own examination. "Trout," I muttered, ready to kill someone. How many times had I told those idiots she didn't do well with fish? And what was Betta doing eating that mess anyway? Lord, she was pale.

Paler than I'd ever been. Paler than... Oh God.

Johnny had been so close tonight. He could have seen any of the pictures in my place. He could have seen her room. We'd almost made love, and when we were done, he'd have had to go to the bathroom to clean up. Betta's bedroom was next to the hall bathroom.

What was wrong with me?

I looked down at her, to the thick bottom lip and the high, arched cheekbones. His features, both of them. My daughter was a Carelli. He'd hate me for never telling him. I'd been with all of them tonight—Cara and Antonia, both my friends. I loved them. They'd never known either. They'd hate me too when they discovered the truth.

One look at her, that heart-shaped face and those round eyes, my eyes—green like my own, like my mother's—and I knew without a doubt, I'd made the right decision. Uncle Patrick had convinced me. The Carellis were good people. But they were not innocent. I couldn't raise a child around that.

I lowered my head, feeling stupid, utterly ridiculous for what I'd gotten myself into. I'd let Johnny back in. I let him talk me into an arrangement for the sake of my charity, forgetting that protecting my daughter was more important than anything else in the world. Even the organization and the kids I loved so much.

"Mama?" I heard, jerking my attention down to the bed and my little girl, staring up at me.

"Hi, baby." I brushed her face, kissing her cheek. "How do you feel?"

"It wasn't my fault." She was immediately anxious, the words rushing out with her quick exhale. "Connie Matthews told me if you took an ibuprofen, you can eat fish even if you're allergic."

"But you don't like fish."

I kicked off my shoes as Betta moved over, making room for me, something she always did when I went in to check on her after she was supposed to be sleeping. She never was. There was always an excuse—a book and a reason she couldn't put it away in favor of the sleep she needed. My daughter was better at fast-talking than her father, God help me.

"I know, but Nathan Miller caught it, and he said he caught it for me. I felt bad for not eating it, even though I told him I didn't like it and he said he understood, I still, well, I felt bad. And *Connie—*" here she rolled her eyes, exaggerating the name like she didn't like how it felt on her tongue "—said I was stupid because Nathan was such a nice boy. And I think Connie likes him, and mainly, I ate it because she called me a coward and I'm no coward."

"No, baby, you're no coward."

Wish I could say the same for myself.

She sat up, looking me over, searching for something I didn't have with me before she took my hands, squeezing my fingers tight. "You're not gonna make me come home with you, are you?"

She was pale, but the quick rush of realization that I might make her come back to the city with me seemed to have put a little color in her cheeks. "You don't want to come home?"

"Well, no. We still have three more weeks. And the volleyball tournament is the last week and I'm team captain and I know we're gonna win." Her eyes were wide, and she looked a little desperate, still holding my hand like she wanted me to understand how important it was for her to stay at the camp. To a nine-year-old, everything in the world was important at that very moment, no matter what that thing may be. The next moment, the next second, would bring the next most important thing. But for now, Betta seemed focused on volleyball and winning.

"Is Connie on the other team?" I asked, guessing her competitive streak had been stoked by more than a game.

"She might be. But that's not why. We've been practicing all summer."

Relief filled me. It seemed far too early for silly things like jealous girls and boys with crushes to be taking up her attention. And by how easily Betta seemed to switch her focus, my worry ebbed. I nestled closer to her, lying on my side so we were face-to-face on the hospital bed. "Okay, but only if you promise not to do stupid things like eat fish just to impress boys or because silly girls call you a coward."

Those big green eyes softened. The familiar thick lips curled into a smile as she lifted her small finger to me for a shake. "Pinkie promise."

"Good." I took the proffered promise and her pinkie before I tugged up the blanket and moved it over her shoulder. "Now, rest. I'll stay with you and then drive you back in the morning."

On the other side of the curtain, I heard the redheaded nurse mumbling something about a shift change, then her instruction to whom I guessed was a new nurse about Betta's condition. When the woman mentioned, "waiting on the doctor to release her," I relaxed, figuring I'd get more details after my daughter had finally gotten some sleep.

"Mama?" I heard, surprised she hadn't dozed off yet.

"Yes, baby?"

"You okay?" I looked down, eyebrows bunched together when Betta frowned at me. "You look sad."

What could I say to that? There wasn't much she'd understand. I'd never mentioned Johnny to her. She'd asked once who her father was, and after Uncle Pat's face had turned four shades of purple, I'd sent him home, promising him I wouldn't tell the girl anything about her father's true identity. I'd made up a small lie about a boy I'd once known, a boy who wasn't ready to be a father.

Does he know about me? she'd asked.

Any man worth his salt would burn down the world to be your father, vita mia.

It was a non-answer she probably never understood, but she never pushed. I suspected Uncle Pat told her something about a boy who was no good. Likely something about never asking me again for fear of breaking my heart. When she was older, I vowed to explain everything. But, nine? No, I told myself, my heart aching as she watched me, concern making her eyes glisten. Nine was just too young.

"I was just worried about my *polpetta*," I teased, knowing she hated the nickname.

Betta's smile was wide, sweet, but it didn't linger on her mouth. She nestled into her pillow, holding my hand against her chest and stifled a yawn. "Don't worry so much, Mama," she said, beginning to doze off. "Everything will be okay. You gotta have faith."

But the only faith I had was stored up in this little girl, and I worried that protecting her wouldn't be an easy job if Johnny discovered who she was.

Chapter Eight
Sammy

My uncle had never quite understood why I refused to marry. Even when I cried against his shoulder, five months gone with a baby and the ink from Johnny Carelli's six-figure apology check long dry, I still wouldn't hear anything about being married off to whatever poor idiot Uncle Pat convinced to have me.

"The baby will be a bastard, my love," he'd said, *patting my head. His voice soft as though the words he spoke didn't sting worse than Johnny swearing he'd never loved me. "It's best you hear the truth."*

I hadn't cared about his truth. "Then it will be my bastard." My uncle could only stare at me when I sat up, my face flushed and wet, my breaths uneven as the life fluttered inside me. "Whoever this baby will be, it will be mine, and maybe one day, when Johnny grows up, when he sees..."

"No." Uncle Pat had always been adamant about that point. There was never any discussion. "You can never tell him. Not any of them." He held my arm, his fingers tightening as he spoke. "My love, whatever else you do, understand this—that family is dangerous. That boy, he is dangerous. Your child will already suffer the indignities of being without a father since you refuse to marry. Better that it have no father at all than one who will put it in danger. An association with the Carellis comes with more trouble than you know."

"But you and Mr. Carelli..."

"I am a servant of the Lord. I am protected. But you, you are carrying one of their own. If they knew, what do you think they would say? A family so protective of their own blood? So determined to pass along that name? Worse than that, what would their enemies do should they discover there is an infant and a young mother who can be bargained with?" Uncle Pat leaned back, removing his wire-rimmed glasses to rub the bridge of his nose. "I know you've convinced yourself that you love that fool boy, but, Samantha, my sweet niece, this cannot be. For the safety of your unborn child, stay away from him and never tell him about the baby." He sighed, staring at me like he knew how harsh he sounded but couldn't keep the words from leaving his mouth. "One day, you'll see. One day, you'll understand that, for this baby, you'll gladly break that boy's heart. You'll break your own if it means keeping it safe."

My uncle hated Johnny. That was no secret. When he'd discovered us, naked in my room four months before, I'd thought he might kill Johnny. I'd never seen Uncle Pat move that quickly or scream that loud. Until he found me throwing up in my bathroom a month later and brought me in to see Dr. Wilson.

"He's ruined you," Uncle Pat promised me.

I hadn't understood how true that was. Even later, at five months pregnant, I still didn't appreciate it. I wanted to make my uncle see reason. Despite how much heartache Johnny had already caused me, telling me he didn't love me, paying off my uncle to keep him from telling his father what had happened between us, I still believed there was a chance. Someday, somehow, we'd come back to each other.

"He'll hate you," my uncle said when I took a breath, readying myself to tell him that the day would come for Johnny and me.

I had faith.

My uncle's once-handsome face was drawn, and he'd seemed to age five years in those five months. Mainly, I thought, because I'd refused to marry anyone or give my baby away. The guilt was often replaced with irritation when Uncle Pat said awful things about Johnny.

Like he did just then. "*I promise you, Samantha. If you tell him you are pregnant after he's promised that he never loved you, his father will force him to marry you. He will obey, but he will resent you. He will always resent you and your child for trapping him. Johnny Carelli is a dutiful son, but he will never be a loyal husband.*"

I hated my uncle that day.

I hated the truth I knew lingered in his words.

I hated that he knew Johnny better than I did.

I moved around my apartment now, staring at more flowers he'd sent me, this time, orchids. They had been waiting for me in the lobby when I returned from Ellenville this morning, signed only with *"Hope everything is OK. Let's finish what we started tonight. Love, J."* And I realized not a lot had changed.

Johnny was still dangerous. With his father gone, that was truer now than ever before. He wasn't some mafia don, as far as I knew, but it wasn't like the Carellis walked the straight and narrow. Cara and Kiel had been shot at last year right in front of her family's museum, and their friend Dale had taken a bullet while they'd hidden in the mountains outside of Seattle because of something Antonia said had to do with "family business," whatever the hell that was.

I couldn't bring my daughter around that.

Besides, once Johnny knew the truth, he'd hate me, just like Uncle Pat promised. He'd never understand why I wanted to keep Betta from him for all these years.

The orchids were purple, my favorite color, something I supposed Johnny remembered me telling him when we were kids. The flowers were delicate but luxurious, something Johnny would understand needed looking after. He counted on me to do the job.

I suppose he counted on me to bend for him too.

To say yes to forgiving him.

To say yes to loving him again.

The bookcase at the back of the room was filled with some of my favorite first editions that I had collected. Some were twentieth-century authors, some older, but among all those books were sporadic frames with pictures of Betta and me over the years. My favorite was of her by herself, her face red and splotchy, her hair pulled back as she spiked the ball in her first volleyball tournament last summer. I'd made it to that camp tournament. She'd performed so well, one of the counselors mentioned an all-girls school in New Haven that Betta would likely flourish at. They had a volleyball team, and I could see her on the weekends. The drive was only a couple hours. It would keep her from Johnny if he wouldn't let me go, or, worse, if he found out what I'd been keeping from him all these years.

I picked up the picture, rubbing my thumb across my daughter's face. I understood the warning my uncle had given me all those years ago. For her, I'd do anything—destroy any shreds of happiness I might have with Johnny if it meant keeping her out of danger. Even if that danger was from her own blood.

The phone rang twice after I selected the number, and with each ring, my chest tightened. I didn't want to make this call. I never wanted to ask the man for anything or to make a confession like this again. But for Betta... Anything for my daughter.

His voice was low, the tone whiskey-rough, and I felt an odd sense of relief just hearing it.

"Uncle Pat?" I said, willing my pulse to slow.

"Sweetheart, is everything okay? How is Betta feeling?"

"She's fine. Just some bad trout." I swallowed down the thick knot of worry that had lodged itself in my throat. I wasn't eager to hear the screaming that was about to come my way. "Listen, Uncle Pat, I need a favor. A big one."

He'd never offered money before because I'd never been this desperate. That was my inheritance, I knew as much, something left to him from his sister, my mother, that my uncle always said would make me a wealthy woman after he died. I'd never questioned him. He was a financial whiz, had grown that nest egg considerably the past thirty years. I trusted him implicitly. But now, I needed his help.

"All right." He paused, and I caught the sound of his leather chair coming through the receiver as he moved. "What can I help you with?"

Best to do it quickly. "I need money, lots of it. To buy out Johnny Carelli."

Chapter Nine

Johnny

The numbers above the elevator took an eternity to rise. Eighty-eight floors and it felt like it took forever for the car to climb. My palms sweated as I watched the ascent, and I couldn't keep myself from messing with the money clip in my pocket. It was a stupid, nervous habit I'd never bothered to lose, but hell, I was an anxious guy.

Except for the call telling me she was stopping by to see me, Sammy hadn't responded to any of my calls or texts since she'd left last night, though I knew she made it home. I'd slipped her day guard a hundred to let me know when she came in and to pick up the orchid I'd sent then shoot me a text to confirm. It was a little sneaky, paying off some guy in her building, but it was damn hard not checking up on her when everything in me told me to make sure she was safe. You couldn't live the life I did and not take precautions, especially with the people you cared about.

And fuck, did I care about Sammy. That much was obvious to me.

Three more floors and my guts felt like melted iron was twisting around them.

Nadine eyed me, but she kept her opinions to herself, typing steadily on her tablet as I rubbed the money clip, top to bottom, then dropped it when the bell above the elevator dinged and the doors opened.

Christ, she was beautiful. Sammy was put together like a Chanel ad in a sleeveless black dress with tight pleats at the waist, showing off her defined biceps, olive complexion, and tiny waist. She wore minimal makeup but smelled, as always, delicious, and she let me take her hand to pull her in for a kiss on the cheek, but nothing more, once she stepped off the elevator.

"Miss Nicola," I greeted, spotting the shift of her gaze as she glanced at Nadine.

"Mr. Carelli." She tugged her clutch purse between her hands when I smiled at her, and that twisting sensation in my gut intensified. "I have some business I need to discuss with you about the center and the renovations." Another slip of her gaze to Nadine, then to my office door before she looked at me. But even then, she didn't linger on my face. "It's urgent."

That got my attention and had me trying to push down the worry I felt collecting in my chest. "Very well," I told her, moving her away from my office and toward another bank of elevator doors across from reception. "Nadine, I'll be in the private quarters upstairs."

"Yes, sir. Shall I hold your calls?"

"Please do," I told her, helping Sammy toward the top-floor elevators.

"Where are you..." she started, still keeping a death grip on her bag.

"There's more privacy upstairs." Sammy followed my motions as I withdrew a key and disengaged the lock pad to call the elevator. "No one will bother us up there." She didn't return my smile or react to the wink I sent her. The worry doubled as I hit the button again, willing the doors to open.

Sammy walked into the elevator without an invitation, keeping her arms crossed and her back straight as we rode up. Through the glass around us, we had a perfect view of the city skyline. Manhattan loomed around us, lit up like Christmas and New Year's all at once just from the building lights and traffic below. But Sammy didn't seem to see anything at all. Her stare was vacant, distracted, something that bothered me more than it should have.

"Here we are," I said when the doors opened. I ushered her into the penthouse, toward the leather sectional at the back of the room.

This was no office, no boardroom, simply a place where we entertained. A bar ran the length of one corner in the back of the room, and several seating areas were intermittently placed around the penthouse. Two hallways in the front and back of the area led to private rooms, bathrooms, and a small kitchenette, but there were no desks and no conference tables. Everything was luxurious—from the marble tiles, lush leather, and high-end fabric of the furniture and area rugs, to the ornate woodwork and modern gold fixtures along the windows and doors. This was a place meant to entice clients and intimidate enemies.

Sammy was neither. But from how she carried herself, how stiffly she walked next to me, I wasn't sure what I should consider her.

"Can I get you something to drink?" I asked, walking to the bar, but I stopped short when Sammy held up her hand, shaking her head with a decidedly sharp movement. "Is there a problem?"

"I just want to get this over with," she said, nodding to the sectional. When I didn't move, Sammy stared at me, narrowing her eyes like she expected more from me.

"What exactly is it you want to get over?" I had my guesses, but I wouldn't voice them.

If I said them, they might come true. Couldn't have that.

"This," Sammy said, retrieving an envelope from her bag. She offered it to me but didn't let me take it. Instead, she slipped it onto the table, pushing it forward like she couldn't stomach the idea of our fingers touching. "This should more than cover the cost of the building and the renovations. I would like to buy my way out of our arrangement."

There was a shake in her fingers that I didn't miss. The tremble moved up her arm, and I swear I caught it twitching across her mouth as she stepped back, gaining distance from the table and the check that lay between us like a bomb. I hoped whatever my expression was, it hid the jackhammering of my heart and the sinking feeling that made me sick to my stomach. This was coming at me out of left field, and it made no sense. Something had set her off since the time we were together, with me deep inside her, ready to take her completely, then that phone call and the mad dash two hours away from the city.

She watched me, seeming to draw strength from the small envelope on the table. The longer it rested there between us, the straighter Sammy's shoulders got and the more confident she became. "Do you have anything to say?" she asked me, uncurling her arms to rest them at her sides.

"Plenty."

It was all I could say, and it was the truth, but I held back, reminding myself what I'd done to her in the past and the promise I'd made to Sammy. I'd do anything for her. Even listen when she wanted to walk away from me.

Instead of arguing when she narrowed her eyes, I held up my hands, hoping to calm her before things got out of hand. I nodded toward the sofa, relaxing only when Sammy eased to the opposite side of the sectional.

I followed her, unbuttoning my jacket before I sat, leaning against the armrest with one arm draped along the back of the sofa and my legs apart. "Now," I said, sizing her up, noting how stiffly she sat, how she held her mouth in a hard line and curled her fingers against her clutch. "Tell me what this is about." Her grip tightened, and I held up a hand, hoping to calm her. "Please."

She swallowed once, back straight, chin moving up, already defiant. "My uncle knows we've been seeing each other."

Some of my worry eased, but I didn't let it show. "Ah."

Sammy was loyal to the old priest, something I understood. He'd raised her. That mean bastard was the only family she'd ever known. He wouldn't take us being together well. It made sense that he'd lay the guilt on her and, being a dutiful niece, she'd listen when he told her to end things.

"So," I said, tapping my thumb against the back of the sectional. "He found out about my helping you with the center and doesn't like it. That forfeits our arrangement, Sammy. There's no need to pay me off."

"No," she said, letting some of the hardness ease from her features, though not for long. She glanced once at me, then rested her bag in her lap, laying her palms flat against it. "Uncle Pat doesn't want you involved...doesn't want us to have any contact. He's adamant and...wants...to buy the building and..."

"What do *you* want?" I knew the answer. I'd read it in her body the night before, when I touched her, when I felt how tightly she wrapped herself around my fingers, around my cock.

She wanted me. She wanted me touching her, tasting her. That reaction, that passion, that sweet, warm wetness, none of it could be faked.

When she didn't answer, I leaned forward, watching how tense she became. She quickly squeezed her eyes closed and held her breath as I sat next to her. "I don't care what the priest wants. I want to know what you want, *bella*."

"That... It doesn't matter." She stiffened when I touched her arm, but she didn't push me away. "Johnny..."

"You want me."

Sammy kept her eyes closed as I watched her, the profile of that beautiful face cast in shadow against the low penthouse lighting and the cityscape outside the expanse of windows around us. She leaned into me when I rested my forehead against her temple and kissed her there.

"I've wanted you since I was a boy."

"It's not that simple." She turned, finally looking at me. "We can't have the things we want just because we want them. There are always other considerations."

"Not for us." This time when I touched her arm, Sammy pulled away.

"*Even* for us." Sammy leaned back, and something descended over her features then, a wall, a veil that told me she would keep herself from anything that made her feel what she wanted for me. "Do this for me," she said, her voice strong but strangled, as though she hated every syllable she uttered. "It's the *least* you can do for me."

My body recoiled at her words just as surely as if she'd punched me. She spotted the reaction I couldn't hide. It was in the wince she released, how she moved her hand, as though she thought of comforting me but then changed her mind in the same second.

Turning, I leaned my forearms on my knees, threading my fingers together, and let the guilt cover me. It burned and poured over every inch of my body, but I welcomed it as the memory of Sammy, so young, so beautiful, her face flushed from her tears, her eyes red and puffy, rushed to the front of my mind.

"I still love you," she promised as I walked away from her. It had been over a year since I'd first broken her heart. She was older, even more beautiful, and she still hadn't let me go.

It took all that I had inside me not to say the words back. She was everything to me then. But I couldn't keep her safe and keep her mine. Not with my father's enemies closing in. Tony DeAngelo had sent his crew to burn down one of my father's factories when Papa finally chose a side and it wasn't his. Four of his men died. Two of the janitor's sons had been killed in the fire, neither one of them older than twelve. Family didn't matter to these assholes. I couldn't keep her safe, not as powerless as I was at twenty.

Sammy's chin shook as I stared down at her, thick, fat tears clinging to her long lashes. Each one acid on my skin.

"I don't love you, Sammy. And I never will."

She stood there in her pink dress, waiting for me to laugh and say I didn't mean it. She would have stood there all night, outside that club with the lowest level of humanity waiting for a fix or attention they'd never deserve or need. But Sammy was better than those people drinking and drugging in that bar. She was better than me, doing my father's business inside it. She always would be.

"I have something to tell you," she said, wiping her face dry.

That was when Olivia McMurry approached the front entrance, and I took the woman for the opportunity she was. "Hey, baby," I called to her, disgusted by her cheap perfume and the stiff texture of her hair from too much product that scratched against my neck when she hugged me.

"Hey, yourself," she said, slipping her arms around my neck.

"Here ya go, kid," I told Sammy, handing her a fifty, not bothering to look away from the overdone

girl in my arms as I spoke. "Make sure you get a cab home."

Of course, she hated me then. She'd gone on hating me for years. I couldn't blame her. Even if I had a good reason, I'd still destroyed all the good we'd had together.

"You still haven't forgiven me." It wasn't a question, and Sammy didn't respond. I went on looking down at my hands, noticing nothing at all but the smell of her perfume and how I wanted to erase everything in the world but her and me and the feel of our bodies coming together.

"Please, Johnny," she said, sounding exhausted. "This is what I need."

"You need him to get his way?"

"I need peace." She lowered her head, rubbing her neck before she exhaled and stood, taking a few slow steps away from the sectional.

"You...you never told me the third thing, Sammy."

She paused, lowering her head, and for a second, I thought she might stop. I followed her, my steps increasing when she moved to the elevator and hit the button. "Tell me about the third reason you fell for me."

"It doesn't matter," she said, hitting the button a second time before she glanced up at the numbers above the car.

"Because I can list a million why I fell for you."

Sammy glanced over her shoulder, not quite staring at me but not looking away either. She rested a palm against the wall, still waiting for the elevator to return, and I didn't bother to tell her it wouldn't come without my key.

"One," I started, taking a small half step, careful not to move too quickly. "The way you cry at the same parts of the same books you've read a dozen times."

She turned farther, finally facing me, but stepped back.

"Two. How loyal you are to the people who mean the most to you, even the selfish assholes you can't see are trying to control you. No one is as loyal as you are, Sammy." I took another step.

She moved back, hitting the wall, her hand coming up to keep me at a distance.

"Three, four, and five. How devoted you are to your beliefs. How passionate you are about the things you love. How you show that passion with everything inside you."

Sammy didn't speak. She didn't argue when I held her face, ready to devour her with one kiss.

"Six. How I know you love me as much as I love you. How I know when I kiss you, you'll kiss me back because it's what you want, and you'll mean it because you don't know how to do anything half-assed."

She let me kiss her, mouth soft and open, compliant as I demanded. Sammy leaned into me, kissing me back, clinging to me as I took everything she offered. It only took a second for her to push away those self-constructed walls, forgetting whatever it was her uncle had said that brought her here. One kiss and another and I had my Sammy back, returning what I gave her, giving me what I wanted.

"There she is," I said, slipping my fingers into her hair, mouth moving down her neck. "Are you back now?"

She released a long, breathless pant, like she was trying to control her breathing as she gripped my collar. "I've always been yours." She sounded winded and a little drunk.

I didn't care; I took what she offered and consumed every morsel. "Turn around."

Something dark and wicked shifted in her eyes, and I grinned, liking that look on her face. The devil surfacing in the angel's gaze before Sammy turned, leaning against me as I moved her hair away from her neck, holding it back in my fist before I kissed along her spine.

"This skin," I said, gripping her hip, loving how she arched against me. How she knew to move with me just how I wanted. "This body..." Sammy bent her head back, leaning into the feeling of my mouth on her neck and my free hand over her stomach, pressing her tight against my hips. "Please, *bella,* don't ever take this away from me."

"I can't..."

Whatever excuse she had ready, I didn't want to hear. I only wanted her right now. Right here. And Sammy seemed to know it. She stopped speaking when I kissed her neck, curling my arms around her waist, moving my hands over her body like I needed to touch every inch of her.

"Don't tell me no," I said, brushing her hair away again to get at her zipper. "Not tonight." Her expression was tense, as though she held her breath, needed to see what I'd do next before she could exhale. I lowered her zipper and pulled her dress down over her shoulders, pushing it to the floor, that tension evaporating. "You can't say no, Sammy," I told her, kissing her skin, licking her spine when I unfastened her bra and threw it to the floor. "Not when your body is so primed for me." She shook against my fingers when I teased her nipples, letting loose a long, breathy moan as I pinched them between my fingers. "Not when I know you're wet for me. You're ready for me." Sammy didn't argue when I moved my right hand over her ribs, tickling her stomach, slipping my fingers under her thong to cup her, my dick getting thicker, harder when I felt the slippery wetness of her slick pussy. "That's for me, *bella?* All that is just for me, *si?*"

She kept silent, breathing growing ragged until I slipped a finger inside her, making her arch against me. She reached up to grab my neck and pulled me down to kiss her. "Johnny..."

"You want me, *bella?* Say so."

"I...want you. I want you now."

"Good," I told her, turning her, holding her close as I walked us both back to the sectional. "Because I want you so much, I can't see straight." Cupping one breast, I kissed Sammy, slipping my tongue deep, holding her thigh on my hip as she moved against me.

She paused when I pulled away from her, a small frown on her face breaking through the lust and heat as I let her leg fall from my hand. It didn't stay there long.

"Turn around, Sammy, and bend over."

It took her a second to think about what I said before she moved, hurrying to situate herself over the arm of the sectional and pull down her thong as I tore off my jacket and tie, untucking my shirt to pull myself from my shorts and pants.

We hurried like two kids. Her leaning forward, waiting, ready; me holding myself and her hip as I angled to meet her from behind until we were together and I slipped inside her, moving slowly, groaning against the sensation of all that heat and tightness I sank into.

"Holy hell..." I muttered, overwhelmed by feeling as I moved. I wanted this to last all night. I wanted nothing more than to be inside Sammy and stay there forever. But I had to move, had to make sure she felt as good as I did. So, I bent her forward, thrusting deep as I slipped my hand around to cup her, teasing her clit, grunting against the feel of her tightening around me and wetting my fingers at the same time.

"Johnny...*ah*... That's good...so good..."

I could have died right there, deep inside this woman, buried in her, with the smell of her around me, touching her, wanting nothing more than to keep this sensation from never ending. Maybe I would have, as long as she'd have me. Sammy rocked back, and I hurried at the sound of her breathing, the little noises she made after just a few minutes telling me she was close.

"This?" I asked her, loving how she nodded as though speech weren't possible. And I moved faster, with my hips, with my hands, gripping her sweet ass, pounding into her, teasing her clit, until wetness covered my fingers and my dick, and Sammy cried out, my name from her lips like a surrender she probably didn't realize she made.

She went limp against the arm of the sectional, and I held her shoulders, angling deep until she arched back, the sensation not complete until Sammy tightened around me, squeezing me. I felt the rise of my climax shoot through me like an electric current.

We staggered away from each other and then back again, curling onto the sofa, naked, exhausted, with Sammy against my chest, her soft, warm breath tickling my chest. I'd never felt more at peace or more worried about what would come later.

The room had gone quiet as our breathing returned to normal, and the only sound I could make out was the low hum coming from the fridge at the back of the room. My entire consciousness was filled with Sammy—the smell of her sweet perfume and the delicious tang of her skin, the warming pant of her breath and the slow tickle of her nails as she ran circles along my ribs. We said nothing. Did nothing but lie there and let the moment take us. It had been ten years since we'd been this way, since we'd been together, and the tingle of the afterglow felt like a high we couldn't get enough of.

"Did I hear you right earlier?" she asked, her soft voice breaking the silence like the rhythm of a tree branch thumping against the ground in a storm. "Did you say you...love me?"

She'd stopped moving her finger over my skin as she waited for me to answer, likely nervous what I'd say. The thought had me grinning. Samantha Nicola, the most beautiful woman on the planet, was scared of rejection. Fucking ridiculous.

"I said I knew you loved me as much as I love you. So, yeah, *bella*. I suppose I did say that."

"Oh." She moved her finger to tease my rib again, a lazy, soothing motion. "Since when?"

Sammy was a smart woman. She'd been a smart girl. I'd spent a lot of years hoping she hadn't been. From the first kiss, she would have known the effect she had on me. Each touch did something to me. Every look, every stolen promise, changed me. I'd wrecked it all, but she was smart. She could see through my lies. It had to be the reason it had taken her so long to let go.

She didn't complain when I turned, positioning her on her back, or when I moved on top of her, needing to see her expression when I made my confession. "Since that first kiss, *bella,* and every kiss after that."

"But you told me..."

"And every day from that first day," I said, covering her mouth with a kiss when she tried to interrupt me. She let me silence her again, taking my tongue until the questions and confusion became too much and she pushed me away.

"You told me you never... You said..."

"I lied. Every single time I told you that, I lied, and I'm sorry, Samantha. I loved you. I still love you. I've always loved you."

Eyes wide, Sammy rubbed the moisture from her lashes, fighting hard to keep herself from crying.

I moved closer, kissing away each tear when it fell. "I'm sorry," I told her, kissing her cheek, tasting the salt from her tears. "I'm so sorry, *amore mia.*" I took her mouth, my thumb stroking over her cheekbone as I stared down at her. "I'll go to my grave protecting you. I'll spend the rest of my life making sure you know how sorry I am that I ever lied to you."

Maybe it was the time we'd spent apart or the lies I'd told that kept us apart. Maybe it was the happiness in that moment of what we might find in the future. But right then, Sammy's tears came quicker, streaming down her face as if from a faucet. She didn't tell me to stop kissing her, and I didn't ask her why she cried. I just leaned over her, taking her mouth, doing my best to show her with my lips and tongue, with every part of my body, that I was hers and I'd never let anything or anyone ever change that again.

Chapter Ten
Sammy

Fairy tales weren't real.

There were no dragons.

No knights coming to rescue the damsel.

I was fine with that. I'd never needed a rescue.

On the day Betta was born, I promised her we'd rescue each other. And we had. Uncle Pat had done what he could, but I had disappointed him. I had shattered all the plans we'd made for my life since I was a little girl because I fell in love and in bed with Johnny Carelli.

But for once, for the smallest moment, I wanted to pretend that the fairy tale could be mine.

Johnny took me to the Hamptons, a magical place meant for only the fantastically wealthy or the fantastically well connected. I'd never been either of those things. Johnny was both.

His family owned a mansion with an oceanfront view, miles from the common tourist traps, with exclusive beach access that promised no one would bother us. There, we would be alone and pretend there wasn't a life and the weight of too much responsibility waiting for us in Manhattan.

At least for a few days.

"Here, there's more pineapple."

"I'm stuffed," I told him, warding off the last few decadent slices of fresh fruit he shoved in my face. He'd spent most of the past hour grilling asparagus and salmon out on the deck while feeding me fruits I'd only seen in magazines and heard about on cable cooking shows.

"Where'd all this come from?" I asked.

He knelt in front of me, lifting the last pineapple chunk in front of my mouth.

I opened wide, laughing when Johnny licked the trickle of juice that slipped down my chin. "Hmm..."

"You'd be surprised..." he started, abandoning the food to inch closer to me. His mouth drifted from my chin and down my neck. "...what you can have ordered last-minute..."

I stifled a moan, still not convinced we were completely alone in this massive home, or utterly secluded from the world despite the private beach being empty.

"...when you've got enough cash."

"Oh."

When Johnny circled my bare nipple with his mouth, I stopped caring about where all the food came from or how private this mansion was and let him divest me of the terry cloth robe. My skin was still pink from a day in the ocean. I was pretty sure I'd never be completely free of sand from between my toes, but Johnny's mouth and tongue and clever, talented fingers were distraction enough that I didn't care about anything but how he made me feel and the small fairy tale we were creating underneath the stars.

It was after midnight when my cell phone rang, and I grabbed it, the fear over Betta gripping me before I realized where I was or who lay next to me naked in this massive bed.

"Hello?"

"Jesus, Mary, and Joseph, Samantha. I've been calling you for two days!"

My skin chilled, and I slipped from the covers, grabbing Johnny's button-up to wrap around my body before I stepped out onto the balcony, not wanting him to hear my uncle screaming at me in the dead of night.

"Uncle Pat," I said once I walked out of the room, realizing the ocean's waves wouldn't do anything to calm me. "Why are you calling so late?"

"Because you damn well wouldn't return my calls. Where the hell are you? Did you give Johnny the check? Have you severed ties with him?"

"Listen…" I started, wincing when I heard the old man's amazed cursing under his breath.

"Have you lost hold of your senses? Dear God, you haven't—" He stopped speaking.

I glanced over my shoulder, frowning when I spotted Johnny sitting up in bed, his arms on his knees as he watched me.

On the other end of the phone, my uncle muttered low, rapid-fire prayers to himself, as though he needed some divine intervention to keep from losing even the smallest grip on his patience. "Did you tell him about the child?"

"What? No, of course not," I said, turning back around and away from Johnny as though he could hear my uncle's question. "You have to let me handle this in my own way and in my own time. Johnny wouldn't take the check. I couldn't force him, and you can't make him sell you the building. It's not that simple."

"Then you'll have to choose another building." Pat's voice was firm and final, as though he'd spoken all he would of the situation and expected me not to argue.

"No," I said finally, ignoring his grunting sigh. "I'm not discussing this with you right now. It's after midnight, and we both need to rest. Stop drinking that whiskey and go to sleep."

"I am not..."

"Priests shouldn't lie, Uncle. Now go to sleep."

I hung up before he could continue arguing, but I couldn't move. Instead, I stared down at the screen, squeezing my phone between my fingers as though that might help relieve some of my anger. It didn't work, and neither did looking out into that low-tide moon. There were too many obstacles laid out before me. Too many hurdles that kept being set higher and higher, and I knew I'd never be able to clear them.

It was all so overwhelming.

Then the balcony door opened, and Johnny slipped out behind me, pulling me to his chest with his chin on the top of my head.

"He's always going to hate me, isn't he?"

"I'm afraid so," I said, figuring there was no reason to sugarcoat anything.

"I'll speak to him when we get back."

I turned, leaning against the railing because I wanted to see his laugh when it came. But Johnny wasn't making a joke.

"What's that look?" he asked, angling his head to the side when I continued to stare at him blankly.

"That would be an exceedingly bad idea."

"Because he hates me?"

I nodded.

Johnny shrugged. "Not for nothing, *bella,* but I think I can handle an old man screaming at me."

"You want to get on his good side? Then stay the hell away from him."

Johnny drew his eyebrows together and tightened his mouth, bringing his lips into a hard line. "I can't do that, Sammy."

"Why?"

"Because." He stepped toward me, resting his hands at either side of my hips on the railing. "You love him, and I love you. Because I want to build a life with you, and he's already in your life. We can't have bad blood between our families. We have to forgive the past if we want a future together."

I felt sick. Something thick and weighted felt like it had taken root in my stomach and settled its claws deep inside me. Now was the time. There would be no better moment. I had to tell him. He had to know the truth.

"Listen—"

"Samantha, I'd do anything for you," he said, interrupting me with his hand on my cheek and his forehead against mine. "I'd kill anyone trying to hurt you. I'd give up every penny I had just to see you smile and, yeah, I'd go crawling to your mean bastard of an uncle, begging his forgiveness for taking your innocence all those years ago. There isn't much I wouldn't do for you."

The phrase struck me as funny. "Isn't much?" I asked, curious.

"Well, I mean, I think I can handle anything but disloyalty. But I don't worry about that with you, Sammy." Johnny straightened, pulling me close.

"You'd never hurt me, I know that." I closed my eyes when he slid his fingers through my hair, shifting my bangs from my forehead and away from my lashes. "I want a life with you. Children...lots of children one day—not now, but one day." That weighted root dug in further, wrapping around my heart and squeezing as Johnny continued. "Smoke, he can take over for me. We've discussed it before. I don't want this life forever, and he doesn't have any ties. When he does, me and you, Sammy, we could make this all...official. We could have everything we wanted. All the things we talked about having when we were kids."

I leaned against his chest, letting the fairy tale wrap around me, already sad because I knew how temporary it would be. "That was a long time ago. Those were big, big dreams, Johnny."

"They were still ours."

They were, but sometimes the dreams we have aren't meant to come true. Sometimes, the dreams of the past are meant to show us the work that must be done in the future. And not everyone is up to the task.

Chapter Eleven

Johnny

Father Patrick Nicola used his office for intimidation. It was a mammoth, ornate space with gothic adornments anyone would expect a priest to surround himself with.

But the old priest had gone a step further, some twenty years back, asking my father to acquire a perfect replica of Hunt's *The Light of the World,* all dark reds and black, with the Christ from Revelation looking menacing and ominous, to hang above his desk. It was an imposing, morose piece, instantly filling whoever looked at it with a swell of guilt and shame that would likely have them itching for a confession.

But I wasn't easily bullied.

No matter that I'd been in this office over a decade before as a punk kid, just discovered naked in

Sammy's bed, unable to look at the old priest for fear I'd be struck dead just by sheer force of his rage for not agreeing to marry her on the spot.

Even back then, though the guilt had been palpable and had lingered ever since, I hadn't allowed the man, or this place, to intimidate me.

I wouldn't today.

"Father Nicola will be with you in just a moment," Sister Dominque said, motioning me to the bench just outside the old man's office. There was a transom above the huge mahogany door, and from the leaded glass, I could make out the gray-green night sky and gold halo of the painting. I heard the irritation in the priest's tone as he yelled at whoever had the misfortune to call him just before he'd been notified that I sat out here waiting for him. Sister Dominque's smile, which was ever-present, faltered only slightly when she heard Nicola's curse after she announced me, but then she shrugged, shot me a wink, and went back to her filing as though the old man's anger wasn't her fault.

And it wasn't. It was mine.

The door flew open just after the sound of a phone receiver rattling against its base reached me, the old priest's face, drawn and wrinkled, hardening as he held open the door and glared down at me. His eyes were sharp and blue, but edged with red, as though he hadn't gotten much sleep as of late. There were bags under his eyes, more than I remembered seeing at my father's funeral a few weeks back.

He didn't acknowledge me, other than to jerk his head back toward his office, stepping out of the way before he cleared his throat, addressing Sister Dominque. "No calls, please."

"Yes, Father." I heard as I walked inside.

I had sense enough to wait for an invitation to sit, which came in the form of a hurried, "Sit," before he moved to his leather chair behind the massive wooden desk.

There were floor-to-ceiling bookshelves surrounding the room and a large fireplace encased in marble and yet another huge religious painting I didn't pay enough attention to identify. Then Sammy's uncle cleared his throat again, bringing my attention back to his desk and the disappointed look on his weathered face.

"Samantha warned me you might be foolish enough to ask to speak with me."

I nodded, weighing my answer and the old man's mood before I spoke. "She advised me not to bother."

"You should listen to my niece. She is remarkably intelligent."

"I know this, Father."

Nicola cringed, but he recovered the expression by opening his bottom desk drawer and pulling out a nearly empty bottle of whiskey, which he didn't offer to share. "She's much more intelligent than you."

"Again," I said, giving him another nod, "this isn't news to me."

"And yet you don't heed her warning and take it upon yourself to darken my door when you know you're not welcome. Why is that, Mr. Carelli?"

I sat forward, pressing my lips together as I watched him pour two fingers of whiskey into a tumbler. "Because there is bad blood between us that I want to resolve."

The priest nearly choked on his drink as he sipped, seeming genuinely amused by my admission. "There is no resolving our bad blood. The wounds run too deep."

"They are old wounds, Father."

"Not to me," he said, humor gone now, pointing at me with his tumbler, one skinny index finger extended. "You were a vile, opportunistic punk who took advantage of my innocent niece, and when I discovered what you'd done, what you destroyed, you shamed her further by refusing to marry her."

"Father..."

"I am *not* your father, Carelli, or your priest."

We stared at each other for more than a minute. The room crackled with tension, and I fought the impulse to knock the tumbler out of his hand and grab the bottle from his desk. I needed a drink and fought the nagging urge to clock the old asshole for dredging up the past, something I'd never be able to change. Something I'd never be able to forgive myself for, no matter what I did.

"What would you have me do?" I asked him, knowing the answer before he spoke it.

"Let her be." He sat back, abandoning his glass for the bottle. "If you really love her, then walk away and let her find someone who will be good for her. Someone who will care for her." He pushed the bottle at me, looking half drunk, half enraged.

"No one can do those things for her like me." I meant it.

One glance my way from him and I understood that the old man knew I was serious. The glare on his face gave him away. He leaned back, one arm flung over his armrest, the other scrubbing over his mouth before he finished the whiskey in one long pull from the bottle.

"Samantha will never marry you without my blessing. And, Carelli, I will never consent to blessing any union between you and my niece." He threw the empty bottle into the trash and leaned back in his chair. "Not ever."

I stood, knowing a losing battle when I was in the thick of one, intent on walking away without a backward glance, until the old man called my name, and my curiosity and some still-flickering hope inside my head had me turning to face him.

"Understand me plainly. If you don't leave Samantha alone, I will make certain there is someone else occupying her time. And make no mistake, she will listen if I suggest they are a better match for her." The priest left his desk, stepping up to me, like he didn't care that I could knock him out with one punch to the jaw. But I was no animal. No matter what he said to me, that he was trying to keep Sammy from me, Nicola was still a priest, and on my worst days, I was still my mother's son and a Catholic. I stuffed my hands into my pockets and repressed the urge to knock the smirk off his face. "Sammy is stubborn, but you know if she is anything at all, it's a loyal, dutiful niece. She *will* listen to me."

I turned, leaving the old man's office while I still held on to my control, trying to remind myself, given the choice, Sammy's loyalty would be with the man she swore she'd always loved. Problem was, I wasn't sure if that was me or her uncle.

Chapter Twelve
Sammy

Some of the renovations had been completed by the time Johnny and I returned from the Hamptons. Indra spent most of the next weekend filling me in on what of the bottom floor was left to complete.

"It all looks so different," I told her, excited to see several of the older students volunteering to help Indra and the staff to organize the classrooms and ready the music room for the upcoming sessions. The ceiling had been fixed and a new air conditioning and vent system installed, and paint and new flooring were over halfway finished on the entire first floor. Blues and greens adorned every wall, and pops of white and black frames accented the surfaces, giving the place a modern vibe that brought a new energy to the whole space. Rico had worked magic, and I was officially under his spell.

There would be an end-of-summer concert next month, and the students were eager to try out the new facilities and, as it turned out, the new equipment and instruments Johnny had purchased as a reopening gift to the center.

"That's because it is different." Indra motioned to the few stragglers. They were all older kids excited about their last concert with the group, watching us as they left the hallway and focused instead on our conversation and not the boxes still left to unpack in the classrooms. "What are you doing?" she asked them, grinning when two of the girls shrugged. One of the older girls, Camille, looked at her companions then smiled, seeming not to care what anyone thought.

She was taller, all knees and elbows, and messy, Indra had always called her, but goodhearted. A mama hen, always taking care of the other kids. But Camille was nosy and she didn't have a filter, something that was apparent as she stepped away from the classroom and rested her hand on her hip, giving me a look that was half tease, half serious inquiry.

"We were just wondering where Miss S's man got off to. He was cute."

"That's enough," Indra told Camille, shooing away the girl and her friends, though she couldn't quite hide her smile. When the girls disappeared into the classroom, Indra turned, arms crossed as she faced me. "That's actually a good question."

"Which is none of your business," I told her, waving her off when she pouted. "Don't make that face. You'll get wrinkles."

"That's not gonna happen." She smoothed a hand over her cheeks. "Too much melanin in this epidermis, my friend."

Ignoring the eye roll I gave her, Indra tried again to dig into my personal business, but she was thwarted when the front doorbell rang. I checked the monitor in the reception area, instantly irritated as I caught sight of my uncle and a man I didn't know waiting outside to be buzzed in.

"Best behavior," I told Indra. My friend frowned, looking toward the entrance as I hit the buzzer, and her frown shifted, morphing into a forced smile that made her look like the Cheshire cat.

"Father Nicola," she said, extending a hand to my uncle.

He took it, accepting the hug she gave him with an awkward pat on her back before he looked over her shoulder, his features relaxing when he spotted me. "Ah, Samantha. Come, please."

The man next to my uncle seemed vaguely familiar, but I couldn't quite place him. He was young, maybe just a few years older than Johnny, with blue eyes and sandy brown hair. He had a dimple in one cheek and wore a tailored blue suit that made his bright eyes shine.

"This is my niece, Samantha Nicola. Sammy, this is Liam Shane." My uncle turned, pushing me toward this Shane fellow with his hand at the center of my back. "Mr. Shane is interested in your charity, love, and wanted to see the facility."

"Your uncle tells me the Carelli family are donors?" Liam asked, a small twitch pulsing over his bottom lip.

"Well, they have participated," Uncle Pat added, dismissing Johnny's involvement in my charity.

"Would you like to see the facility?" I asked Liam. I felt awkward and on edge that his first question had been about Johnny's family. He nodded once, and Indra greeted him, bringing him into one of the classrooms.

"You should be in there with him, not your friend," Uncle Pat said, leaning close to me as though he didn't want anyone to make out what he said.

"Why? It's not like..." I turned, only just noticing his smile. My stomach fell, and I took a step back, head shaking. "What are you doing? My Lord, you know this isn't going to work."

"You deserve someone respectable, and this Shane fellow is an attorney from a good family. His father owns several trucking companies, and he has his own money as well. You could do worse, and he's better than..."

"Than what, Uncle Pat?" I stepped closer, pulling him away from the hallway and the classrooms. "Better than the father of my child? Where is this even coming from? Johnny told me last night that he went to your office and you both agreed..."

"We agreed? What did that boy say we agreed to?" His voice was loud now, indignant, and he didn't lower it when I tried to quiet him. "Tell me."

"Johnny said you agreed to disagree about us being together but that you would...stay...out of it." Saying it aloud made it sound idiotic. My uncle couldn't stay out of my life any more than I'd ever be able to keep from advising Betta on anything, regardless of how old she got.

Once you're a parent, you're a parent for life.

I dropped my shoulders as the swell of anger and disappointment bubbled in my gut. Johnny had lied to me. It might have been in an effort to give me at least a little peace, but it was still a lie no matter the intention.

My uncle's unamused laugh felt like a slap across the face, all bitter and irritating, and I stepped back, waiting for him to deliver the final insult. "Agreed to disagree. That stupid boy wanted my blessing."

"And you said?"

"The truth." He frowned, acting disappointed, as though I should have guessed his response. "I will never give my blessing for you to be with Johnny Carelli. You have always known this. Now, he does too."

Behind us, Indra's voice carried as she led Liam back toward the lobby.

"He has money and wants to donate," my uncle whispered, holding my arm as he turned me to face

Liam. "If he invites you to dinner, accept. There's no harm in keeping a man like that company after he's donated handsomely to your charity."

"No, I suppose there isn't," I said, wanting to be anywhere other than in this building, facing this man. He was handsome enough, but he wasn't Johnny. No one ever would be, no matter who my uncle decided I needed to be spending time with.

"Ms. Nicola, the facility is excellent. Tell me, how big is your staff?" Liam asked, nodding as he looked around the room.

"Ah...we host a staff of fifteen volunteers," Indra offered for me when I didn't answer the man quickly enough.

"Yes," I finally said, still in a bit of a daze from the information my uncle gave me. I didn't like how Liam seemed to calculate square footage or how closely he watched our teachers and students breaking down tables and chairs and reconfiguring their placement in the rooms.

"Well, I'd love to discuss a donation and the possibility of a fund raiser I have in mind over dinner. Say, tonight at eight?" Over Liam's shoulder, my uncle nodded, throwing me an insistent, encouraging nod of approval.

"Eight tonight?"

"Yes," Liam said, stepping closer to take my hand. He held it to his mouth, kissing my knuckles longer than I thought was necessary or comfortable. "Eight tonight. Just you and me, Ms. Nicola."

"Like hell," Johnny said, stepping through the front entrance doors as they closed behind two exiting volunteers. His face was contorted in twisted anger. He bypassed my uncle, who tried and failed to stop Johnny from approaching me, and went straight for Liam, standing in front of me as he tore the man's hand from my fingers. "You're gonna want to back the fuck up, Shane."

"Carelli," Liam said, laughing as though Johnny weren't glaring at him like he was ready to do him serious damage. "I'm sorry, did I step on your toes by coming here?"

"You know where you are, and you know why the fuck you shouldn't be."

"Do I now?" Liam stopped smiling and dropped his hand, slipping it into his pocket as he stared up at Johnny. "I got no reason to cause beef with you."

"No? But you got pissed that Cara's husband put you out on your ass the other night, and I hear you've been asking around about them. When that got you nowhere, you started asking about me and mine. You being here—" he nodded, motioning toward me "— makes me think you're itching for a scrap, when you know damn good and well you don't want that shit."

"Johnny, please stop..." I said, but he held up his hand, silencing me without even a backward glance.

"I think," Liam started, not backing down or cowering away from Johnny as he kept his stance wide and intimidating. "You got territorial issues where they don't belong. According to Father Nicola, you have no business here. I do." Liam bit his bottom lip, tilting his head toward me, nodding twice. "I'll admit, maybe I've got words for your cousins about things I'm owed." He slipped his gaze to me, looking me over like I was naked and he liked what he saw. "But this? Bonus. And I plan to make that shit my *personal* business."

It was a threat enough for Johnny to act, and when he did, the result wasn't pretty. One small shove set Liam off. Johnny seemed to allow the man the first swing, but the first one was all it took before Johnny blocked him, clapping him on the ear loud enough that the sound echoed around the room, and Liam grunted, covering his injury. Johnny pushed his advantage, punching into the man's gut, sending him to the floor.

"Johnny! Stop it right now!" I tried, only to be held back by both my uncle and Indra when I made a pointless attempt to separate the two men from spilling blood in front of my kids. "Oh God," I said, spotting a few of them staring out of the slightly open classroom doors as Johnny and Liam fought. "Get in the classroom!" I told them, and they scattered, still peeking through the windows and the doors.

"That...all...you...got..." Liam said, throwing a dirty punch that caught Johnny on the right side of his jaw.

Johnny seemed tired of the tussle and blocked a second attempt before he jumped on top of Liam, pinning down both his arms before he started to slam his fists into Liam's face over and over again.

"God!" Indra said, hurrying out of the building and running toward Angelo, Johnny's guard, who was leaning against the Mercedes parked outside our building.

"You see, Samantha?" my uncle started, pointing at Johnny as Angelo charged inside and pulled the men apart. "This is all he will ever be. Nothing more than a thug. You deserve better than him."

Johnny turned, his knuckles bloody, the underside of his jaw cut and already bruising. He didn't stare at me. Instead, he shot my uncle a glare, his features tight and menacing before he shook his head, looking like he needed a moment to remind himself he wasn't supposed to throttle men of the cloth.

"He won't ever change—" Uncle Pat tried, but I cut him off, stepping away from him and the look on Johnny's face as he watched me.

Uncle Pat's anger lingered, got tied up in what I knew looked like Johnny's defeat. I'd seen it before. I'd put the same expression on his face a dozen times in just the past weeks alone.

I broke away from my uncle's grip, ignoring that frustrated look. I also ignored my uncle's voice as he called after me, and I spared one final glance at Johnny before I left through the front door.

"Please...take care of my kids," I told Indra, passing her as I walked out the door. "I've gotta go..."

"Yeah, Sam. Go," she said, practically pushing me out of the building.

I tried to forget the regret that had doubled. Now I wasn't sure if Johnny was disappointed in me for walking away or worried that I wouldn't come back.

Chapter Thirteen
Johnny

You can't own a woman.

She isn't your property.

She isn't your possession.

But *she* can completely control *you*.

It was the only answer for how consumed Sammy made me feel—half crazed, half possessed by the worry that she'd walk away and I'd never get the chance to earn her forgiveness or her love.

I lied. She had to know about that shit by now. Why else would she bother giving a piece of shit like Liam Shane a second glance? Sammy had no idea who or what he was, and I had a sneaking suspicion him being at her center had all the hallmarks of her uncle's interference.

It all came down to the old man and the games he was playing with Sammy's life. I used to think, once he was gone, the problems between us would be over. But that wasn't true. People like the priest left marks. They left shadows that could never be erased. He was making sure the shadow he left behind would eradicate me from Sammy's life.

I just couldn't let that happen.

She was angry. I got that. She'd likely be angrier knowing I'd ditched Shane and her uncle at the center and tailed her back to her temporary offices after Indra sent the volunteers and kids home. I gave Sammy time enough to cool off. Time enough so that when I showed, she wouldn't want to throttle me. But when I walked into the lobby, the place was empty. No Sammy. No funny Indian friend of hers always cracking jokes.

Then I heard their voices coming from the back of the building, from the location of the small kitchen area Antonia had shown me when I'd toured the building. The first thing I could make out clearly was the clinking of glasses, then liquid pouring. Hell, it seemed we always drank when shit got rough, and shit was *always* rough of late.

I stopped just before the doorway, catching Indra's and Sammy's reflection in a framed list of class schedules against the wall. The women sat at a small table, their feet resting on chairs opposite each other with two wineglasses and a full bottle of wine between them. Sammy had pulled up her long hair, and from her reflection, I could make out how tired she looked, how worn down she was by the day, likely by the shitstorm I'd caused in her life just from pursuing her.

"You love him, don't you?" Indra asked, and I held my breath, hoping that much hadn't changed since the last time Sammy had told me she loved me.

"I love him." Sammy nodded, the soft, slow smile on her face easing some of the worry that made my chest tighten at her friend's question. But then the smile fell away, and she leaned on the table, rubbing her neck like she hated admitting that out loud. "Sometimes I hate him, you know?"

"It's the nature of the beast. Can't live with them..."

"Can't shoot them."

"Well," Indra said, smiling behind her glass, "that depends on where you live."

Sammy nodded, lowering her shoulders, her eyes taking on a glassy, out-of-focus stare. "I just know when I'm with him, everything makes sense. I feel like..." She went quiet, her chin shaking, but she made no noise as that sheen in her eyes grew thicker and she started to cry. "I feel like...myself."

"And when you're not?" Indra reached across the table, grabbing Sammy's hand and holding it.

Sammy took the comfort until she pulled away. "Then I remind myself of all the nights I lay in my bed knowing what it felt like when Johnny Carelli ripped your heart out."

I leaned back against the wall, eyes closed as I let Sammy's words rush over me. I didn't need to see her expression. It had played in my head a thousand times over the last ten years.

Her crying as I told her I didn't love her.

"So, that doesn't answer my question," Indra said. "What do you want?"

Her face red and blotchy, sniffling while she stood on that sidewalk, holding a fifty-dollar bill in her hand as I walked away with some tart on my arm.

"I want to be happy and not have to worry if the man I love is going to come home or not." Sammy wasn't telling Indra anything she didn't know about my family.

Everyone knew who we were. It was why her uncle had always warned her away from me, she'd confessed. Friendships with a Carelli were fine. Love was not.

"I want a family and to have lots of babies and to be with a man I never get tired of kissing." Sammy's voice was softer now, like the thought of a happy life filled her from the inside out. I hadn't heard her speak that way in years. "I want that feeling to last forever." She released a long, rough breath, and when she spoke again, that soft tone was missing from her words. "Is that too much to ask?"

"Of course not."

"But I can't stay away from him, even though I know I should. For my own sanity, I should."

She should. I knew that. We both did. Liam Shane had hinted at a beef today that wasn't mine, but it belonged to Smoke's family. My family. My blood. Shit like that would probably always touch me. It would never be far enough away from me, no matter where I went.

Could I protect her from that? Would she ever be safe?

"I just want to feel normal and secure," Sammy told Indra, sounding desperate. It was what I wanted for her too. "I just want to be happy for once in my pathetic life." She was miserable now because of me. Would she always be? "I just...want to be happy."

Pushing off the wall, I walked away from the kitchen and the sting of Sammy's words. The truth hurt worse than any lie. But sometimes, the best thing we could do caused the most pain, especially when they were the hardest sacrifices we ever had to make.

Chapter Fourteen
Sammy

There were two missed calls and a text message on my cell when I finished drying my hair after a long shower. I was torn between wanting to hear Johnny's voice and swearing off him forever.

Each choice seemed logical.

Each seemed ridiculous.

Both were pointless.

Johnny hadn't called.

Angelo had brought over pizzas and movie tickets for the kids and volunteers as a way of apologizing for causing a scene. He'd even sent "Mr. Carelli's sincerest apologies" to me personally with a bottle of red and more roses, but Johnny himself had not called.

Most of the day, I'd decided on the "swearing off him forever" option and screened my calls. The missed calls, I guessed, could be him. But as I finished brushing my hair, deciding I'd take Indra up on her offer of dinner and a movie, partially on Johnny's dime, and I grabbed my cell, I noticed neither the calls nor text had been from Johnny. The 845 area code was Ellenville, and I immediately selected the message, spotting the camp number, and dialed it.

Betta picked up on the second ring. "I'm okay, Mama. I promise," she said, sounding a little stuffed up.

"Do you have a cold?"

"No." She exhaled, and the sound put me on alert. That was no "exhausted kid" sigh. That was an emo, "in my feelings" sigh that my kid knew to use anytime she wanted to bend my ear.

"What's up, baby? Did something happen?"

"It's just...Connie..."

"I'm starting to really not like this kid..."

"Yeah, me too, Mama." Betta cleared her throat, and I picked up the sound of a screen door shutting, as though she'd moved to a quieter location. "She's a turd, I swear."

"Elizabetta, even if she is, that's impolite." She was quiet for a second too long, and I laughed. "Okay, why specifically is she a turd now?"

"She told the entire camp I'm an orphan."

"Which is ridiculous. You have my eyes."

"I know," she said, her voice rising in her excitement. "And I even showed them my locket with your picture and Granny's and was all, 'See, my eyes are just like my mama's and her mama's. And you all saw her bring me to camp, so you don't know what you're saying.'"

"Good. That's good, baby. I'm glad you stood up for yourself."

My chest tightened, and I had to force back the bubble of filthy words that wanted to fly out of my mouth. Lord, kids could be cruel, and the worst aspect of being a parent was that you couldn't fight your children's battles. You want to. You're equipped. You could destroy those little cretins, but you have to let your kids fight for themselves. It was the worst sort of irony.

"Yeah, well, it didn't work all that well because Connie laughed in my face and told everybody I might have a mama, but even I didn't know who my father was."

I closed my eyes, hating myself, hating Johnny, and really hating this stupid little Connie brat for being so vicious. "Oh, baby…"

She didn't speak, not for a long time, and I'd never felt more powerless as I did just then, listening to my nine-year-old daughter sniffle and cry on the phone, pretending she wasn't heartbroken that I'd never told her anything remotely useful about the man who'd helped make her.

"Mama," she said finally, her voice cracking, each sound like a knife into my heart. "Do you think, one day soon, you can tell me...about...*him?* Not...everything, not if you can't... If it's too... Uncle Pat said...well. But maybe something..."

"You have his smile," I told my daughter, unable to keep the emotion out of my voice.

"I...I do?"

"Yeah, baby. And it's beautiful."

The rectory had once been a barn. The building was a century old; the Church had purchased it years back, and priests like my uncle had lived under its roof for generations. But, if memory served, Uncle Pat had been here the longest.

There were mementos of his life everywhere. In the bookshelves surrounding the small den and along the fireplace. There was no television, only a small radio and a stack of papers near the front entrance to keep him abreast to world events. Bibles and religious texts were placed around on the shelves and open on the coffee table, on the small desk in his private office and atop the dining room table. But among them was evidence of his personal life too. His family—a framed picture of Betta and Uncle Pat at her first communion with her wearing the same dress I'd worn at mine. He'd confirmed us both. All three of us at the Vatican when Betta was six, getting a blessing from the Pope, something Uncle Pat had been adamant about.

And above the mantel in the den, there was a large portrait of my beautiful mother, Uncle Pat's sister, on her eighteenth birthday. Hints of our lives were everywhere, connected to the world in which he was a man of God, someone who was supposed to be pious and forgiving.

I prayed he'd remember that when I delivered my news tonight.

"You want wine?" he asked, setting down the book he'd been reading when I walked through the door. He still had an attitude, and I suspected he hadn't quite forgiven me for leaving him with Indra to sort out the mess Johnny and Liam Shane had made at my center.

"If you have an open bottle. If not, don't bother."

He ignored me. I watched him, his body hunched more now than it had been even a year ago. My uncle was edging closer to seventy-five, and time and his responsibilities had accelerated his aging.

"I can do that," I offered, walking toward the kitchen, but Uncle Pat made a noise, dismissing me, and handed over my glass before I crossed the threshold.

"Sit," he said, motioning with his chin to the couch. He moved to his armchair, shifting against the thick cushion as he rested both elbows on the armrests and held his glass in his hands. "Now..." He took a sip, closing his eyes as though he wanted to enjoy the flavor of the drink as it hit his tongue. "Tell me."

"Elizabetta called me this afternoon." Uncle Pat kept still, his eyes narrowing as he waited for me to continue. "She was upset because the kids at camp were teasing her..."

"Kids can be cruel."

"They were teasing her because she has no father."

He didn't move but watched me closely, his features frozen as if something had taken over his body and immobilized him. "And?" he finally said, setting down his glass on the side table at his left. "What did you tell her?"

My uncle could be intimidating. He was strong. He was intelligent, and he had a vicious temper when angered. He was never cruel, not to me, but if you crossed him, disobeyed him, or worse yet, disappointed him, that temper would surface, and forgiveness wouldn't come easily.

As a child, that temper petrified me. I only wanted to please him, make him proud. I wanted to be the best, do the best because I craved his approval. That had left me making promises I didn't mean, swearing myself to a destiny not meant for me. That was probably why I'd clung to Johnny so tightly. Not only because I loved him, but because he showed me a freedom I never thought could be mine.

I wasn't a child anymore. It was time my uncle understood that.

"I told my daughter the truth." Uncle Pat sat up straighter, clutching the end of the armrests, but I didn't let him intimidate me or interrupt my explanation. "Not everything, but some of it." Then I matched my uncle's posture, fixing my shoulders straight, lifting my chin to watch his eyes when I finished what I had to say. "Johnny Carelli is not a perfect man, but no one is. I have loved him since I was a girl, and I have never stopped loving him." My uncle stood, jaw clenched, top lip shaking. Still, I continued. "We made a beautiful, perfect baby together, and she deserves to know the reason she's never known who she is. They both may hate me for it, but I intend to tell them everything."

He clenched his fists into balls, squeezing them so tightly his knuckles went white. I stood, hoping he would calm, hoping he would try to see reason. He was supposed to know forgiveness and mercy. He was supposed to show compassion, but he'd never had any of those things for Johnny.

"Uncle..."

"When?" he said, the word coming out from behind his gritted teeth. I tilted my head, not understanding what he meant, and Uncle Pat flared his nostrils, holding his head in one hand before he clarified. "When will you tell that...*that*...boy about Elizabetta?"

"Tonight, maybe? Or...tomorrow? I want to tell him first, before she gets back from camp next week."

He closed his eyes, his face flushing red.

"Uncle Pat..."

But he ignored me, lifting a hand to silence me as he stumbled away from me and toward the fireplace, resting against the mantel. He moved his attention to the portrait of my mother, muttering to himself, his pale skin redder and redder the heavier he leaned against the mantel.

"Uncle Pat?" I tried again, my heart racing when he continued to wave me away, refusing to look at me, then he fell, his small, weak frame crumpling as he landed on all fours. "Oh God! Oh my God!" I ran to his side, feeling his skin, my breath catching when I noticed how hot he was to the touch.

"Samantha..." he whispered, falling onto his back. He reached for me, touching my face with his scorching palm, his bright eyes fluttering before they closed and he lost consciousness.

Chapter Fifteen
Sammy

There is nothing more silent than a waiting house. It comes from death and from homecomings when babies and soldiers return. It comes from reunions that are long overdue, but always, there is the quiet until the moment of arrival.

Tonight, there was only me and this old home, haunted by the ghosts of a hundred priests. We were all waiting for my uncle to heal, to recover.

"It was a massive heart attack, Ms. Nicola. We've made him comfortable, but we won't know the extent of the damage until he wakes up." The doctor had been kind and thorough, but his tone wasn't hopeful. *Until he wakes* up felt a lot like *if he wakes up*.

"What can I do?" I'd asked, desperate for some occupation that kept me from pacing the ICU hallway, wondering how many hours I had left until I could sit next to my uncle's bed to watch him breathing, lying there, looking lifeless and old. "Please," I'd asked, not caring how pathetic I sounded. "Tell me what to do."

"Rest," the doctor suggested, and when that didn't elicit more than a frown from me, the man lowered his shoulders and touched my arm. "Go to his home. Find a book you know he'll enjoy, and bring it back here. Maybe reading to him will help you both."

I knew busywork when I saw it, but at least there was something to do now that didn't end with me aimlessly counting the watermarks on the hospital's tile ceiling.

There was a nonfiction book about the assassination of Abraham Lincoln on the coffee table. I glanced at the cover, frowning at the writer's name across the center, then went into my uncle's office, figuring he still kept his collection of John Donne poetry and sermons in the same place.

"Comfort and conscience," he'd told me as a child, showing me the worn book, the edges rubbed down and pages dog-eared after years of use. "That is the message Donne delivers."

The desk was small, modest, and very old. It had been handed down to him from an old bishop he'd studied under at monastery, and he'd brought it with him to every parish he'd served. It was solid and thick, with a bank of drawers on both sides and a small thin drawer in the center. I sat behind it, immediately opening the right-side center drawer, where I knew he kept his favorite Donne collection. The swivel chair squeaked as I turned, flicking on the desk lamp when I didn't spot the book in the drawer. There were small journals and boxes of pens, a few bundles of stamps, and two stacks of index cards, but the Donne wasn't in the drawer.

The bottom drawer was locked when I tried it, and the others gave me nothing but more of my uncle's journals, a few random envelopes of pictures from his tenure at Trinity College, and several bookmarks from book readings I knew he'd attended, but still, no sign of the Donne.

Then, just as I decided to give up and I reached across the desk to turn off the lamp, I spotted a sliver of gold peeking out from underneath and moved it aside. The lamp had a heavy base with two small openings on either side, and beneath the opening closest to me, taped to the base, was a small key. I grabbed it, my heart beating double time, wondering what secrets my uncle had kept that seemed important enough to hide.

A thousand scenarios raced through my mind, none of them good. There had been surprises coming from gossiping mouths in every church—people you knew for years, doing despicable things, so you never quite knew who to trust. But my uncle had never given anyone any reason to gossip about him. He'd always been transparent. He'd always been open with his parishioners and bishops. There simply wasn't anything to hide.

So why was that drawer locked tight?

I slipped the key into the lock, turning it with one twist, and I held my breath before I opened it, my heart somewhere near my throat by now, my breathing coming in wild, uneven pants.

At first, there seemed to be only the brown leather book with gold lettering. It was familiar, like the one I'd seen my uncle hold for years as he read through each poem and sermon penned by the English poet. There was nothing suspicious about the book, nothing that would warrant being locked inside this drawer. So I grabbed it, not bothering to look at it, more focused on what else was hidden—a manila envelope with a typed name and date, NICOLA, AVA R. 10/01/1991.

My mother's name and my birthdate? He'd never let me see my birth certificate. Said it had been lost years ago. I'd always suspected he worried I'd ask about my father and he never wanted me to know.

Funny how history repeated itself.

Not funny at all how I allowed my uncle to convince me to do the same thing to Betta.

The certificate itself held no surprises other than to note that my mother had been thirty-five when she'd had me. I'd always assumed she'd been younger. Uncle Pat had told me very little about their family. I'd never met cousins or grandparents; all, he'd said, had abandoned my mother for having a baby with no husband to speak of and him, for supporting her. No father was listed, but the time and place of birth were odd. My uncle promised our people had all been born and reared in New York. Generations, he said, of Italian Nicolas went back decades in the city.

So why was my mother's birthplace listed as New Orleans?

The only other things in the folder were two pictures. One was of my mother and me in the delivery room. It was a typical early-nineties image, the pigmentation was bright, the scrubs colorful, but the smile on my mother's face was wide, and her green eyes shone like wet glass as she smiled at the camera. She was beautiful, and a lump caught in my throat as I touched her face. I stared at that picture a long time, willing all that light and ink to come to life, just for a second, so I could know all her secrets, to find out everything I could about her.

After a while, with my eyes blurring, I put the picture away, picking up the second photo, confused when I spotted another delivery room image, this one of my mother and me again, but joined now by my uncle, decked out in blue scrubs. It struck me as weird somehow that my modest uncle, who'd had to ask Sister Dominique to discuss tampons and menstrual cycles with me when I was eleven, would be a man comfortable enough to be in the delivery room when his sister gave birth.

The picture was striking and...oddly intimate. The way he leaned close to her, his arms around her shoulders, him cradling both of us, looking fierce, like only he could protect us. A mix of consuming thoughts worked inside me—confusion, curiosity, and a real sense of wonder that there was something I was missing. Something significant enough that my uncle thought it should be locked away in his desk.

The Donne book felt heavier when I picked it up, though it had been years since I'd held it. It was the same book I'd seen my uncle read a dozen or more times; it had the same binding, the same red-tinted edges on the pages from the time I'd spilled Kool-Aid over it at nine and didn't clean it properly.

Inside, though, a new world opened to me that had nothing to do with Donne or the sweet words he'd penned about love and sin or the sermons promising repentance for his misdeeds.

The first letter was old. There was no address, no stamp at all, and the envelope was folded, the looping handwriting across the front carrying what looked like the carefully constructed letters that made up my uncle's name. No "Father," no "brother." The envelope and the letter inside simply stated "Patrick."

She loved him.

He loved her.

One letter became two, then five, then ten, and as I sat there for hours, reading these impossible, unbelievable words, the story of my parents' life unfolded.

She'd been a parishioner in his church. A shy, timid woman with a strict father eager for her to marry. When she'd worked up the courage to refuse, he'd sent her to the new priest, hoping someone closer to her age could make her see reason, could convince her of the importance of obedience.

It had backfired.

I think of you, my mother wrote in the first letter, and my heart broke for her. My hands shook as I imagined what it had been like for her, remembering what it felt like to love someone so much...but be made to keep it deep inside yourself. *I think of you always, with every waking breath and every blissful dream. I pray that God takes this love I feel for you from me. I pray not to want you. I pray that I will hate you. I pray for freedom from all the thoughts I have of you. It's the same prayer I've said for two years now. Will He ever answer me? Will He ever let me be free of you?*

Patrick's letters were stronger, but his patience didn't falter. He started them with Donne.

> *I am two fools, I know,For loving, and*
> *for saying so.*
> He let the poet say more in two lines
> than he could in one.
> *My sweet Ava, God has my promise,*
> *but you own my soul.*

I read the last letter, dated just eight months before I was born. They had a plan, put into action before any of my mother's family knew she was pregnant. In the end, she would not let him leave the Church. She would not let him sacrifice his calling for her.

Who am I to ask you to choose between your devotion to God and your love for me? Instead, I only ask that you stand by me, that you give what you can to me and our child, whatever that may be. God would not be so cruel as to damn a perfect soul made from the love He has borne between us.

Patrick had done exactly what she wanted. He had never married her, but she had his name. So did I. Had he lied to his bishop? Had someone forged documents for them? They left New Orleans when he was transferred, which, from the last letter I read, came in time that no one would know of my mother's condition. They'd hidden from her family and moved to New York, posing as brother and sister. My entire life, I'd been told that my mother had married a man on a whim, some local she'd met while on vacation in Rome. But he left her after a month, and she returned home to New York, already pregnant, with no idea where her husband had gone.

But it had been a lie.

All of it.

Everything I knew.

Everything I believed my entire life had been constructed to protect a man from the same sin he'd never forgiven me for making.

I dropped the book, the letters and pictures falling to the floor around me, and I threw back the chair. The air in the room had become too thick, the staleness of this old place suffocating me until I thought I might pass out.

I needed to get out, away from the rectory, from my uncle's secrets, from anything that reminded me of the lies told to keep me under someone else's control. The street was crowded when I hit the sidewalk, but I managed to hail a cab immediately, slipping inside before I could get my heartbeat to slow.

"Where to?" the driver asked, and I called out the address, thinking of the only place in the city with the only person who'd ever made me feel any real freedom. I'd go to him and try to forget for just one more night that my world was falling apart.

Chapter Sixteen
Johnny

She was a drug I needed out of my system.

The smell of her hair, the warmth of her skin, the feel of her nails against my back when I moved inside of her—it was all better than any drink, than the sweetest bump I'd ever taken.

Sammy was addictive, and I was going on day five without a single fix.

Angelo watched her, made damn sure no one, especially not Liam Shane, touched a hair on her head. Last he'd reported, she'd been with her uncle at the rectory.

No harm, no foul, and I told him to call it a night.

My apartment was too quiet. The empty rooms, the vacant noise of nothingness... I just couldn't be there. So, I told myself work would give me something to do. It would fill the monotony. It would distract me from the withdrawals I had from not seeing Sammy, not hearing her voice, not tasting her mouth.

But an hour in and I was already listless. The projections were done. The figures figured. No meetings could be had on a Friday night at eleven p.m. Garcia had been called and handled. I exaggerated about the trip to the Hamptons with Sammy, let him think we'd extended it so he wouldn't get suspicious.

Everyone else had a family.

Everyone else had a life.

Mine had passed me by.

I shot tequila straight, not bothering with a glass. No need for propriety when there was just me and my damn internal whining as I watched New York below me, moving along, going forward, while I waited for Samantha to leave my system.

Then, as if I summoned her with some spell, the elevator chimed. Angelo ushered her in, knocking once on my door before he opened it, holding it ajar long enough for Sammy to march inside. One look at her face and I knew shit had tumbled for her.

"What happened?" I said, moving away from the window to meet her in the middle of the room.

She was mad; that much I could see—eyes wide and wild, bloodshot and red. Her normally smooth, wavy hair was in disarray, and her clothes were wrinkled, like she'd slept in them. Sammy opened her mouth to speak, then glanced over her shoulder, eyebrow cocked as she looked at Angelo.

"It's okay, man. I got it," I told him, nodding for him to close the door.

She barely let the latch close before she rounded on me. "Your father, did he know? Did he tell you?"

"Tell me what?" I set the bottle on my desk, touching her shoulders, hoping that would calm her. It only seemed to make her angrier.

"About my... About Father Patrick? Did your father know about him and my mother?"

"What about them?"

The frown she gave me was severe and misplaced.

I'd done a lot to deserve her anger but nothing in the past few days. If she was pissed at me, I wanted it to be for something I knew I did. "*Bella,* is this about me exaggerating what he and I..."

"What I'm asking you, Johnny Carelli, is if your father ever told you that he knew Patrick Nicola wasn't my uncle? Did he tell you that Patrick and my mother were not brother and sister?" She walked to my desk, pulling out of my reach to grab the bottle. In all the time I'd known her, I'd never seen Sammy drink tequila. Wine, often, sometimes whiskey, but never tequila and never straight from the bottle.

"Sammy..."

"What I want to know—" she chugged, squeezing her features as she shook off the taste "—is if you knew that Patrick is my...father."

"I..." My head swam, and I couldn't do much more than watch her, trying to make sense of whatever nonsense had just left her mouth. "What?"

"Yeah..." Another swig, this one deeper.

It made sense now—her shock, her appearance, her loss of calm and control, and the immediate need to dull whatever pain must be riddling her. I couldn't even imagine what that would feel like...being lied to by the one person you thought could never hurt you.

"Sammy..." She silenced me with a headshake, and I moved to her, still only able to stare, still too shocked to do anything but watch her and only because I couldn't think of anything else to do. I grabbed the tequila from her and took one long pull, wiping my mouth dry with the back of my hand.

"Come on," I told her, grabbing her hand to bring her to the sofa next to my desk. "Tell me what happened."

"He had a heart attack after we..." She went quiet, and I knew there was something she didn't want to share. Something I wouldn't push her to tell me. Sammy had always kept her secrets. That likely would never change. I respected that. Being who I was, in the family I was in, I understood the value of a secret, so I let it lie and just listened. "He got upset when I told him that I wouldn't...cut you out of my life." She seemed calmer now, but the tears began to surface. She didn't lean on me when I moved closer to her side, and I figured she was still angry about the mess I'd made of Liam at her center.

"I went to the rectory to find a book for him... He likes Donne. And I found..." Sammy rubbed her face, wiping it dry quickly, as though she couldn't stomach the tears and how quickly they came. "The letters between them. My mother and him. He was her priest, and she loved him. He loved her back and she wouldn't let him leave the Church and I'm a bastard... All this time..." She stiffened before she stood up, pacing around my office. Whatever she kept to herself seemed to buzz around her head like an insect keeping her quiet but distracted, like she was trying to work out her own shit and didn't need me to help her.

I couldn't help myself. I just couldn't see her like that.

"Sammy, please..." I tried, stopping her with my hands on her arms. "You're pissed off, and you have every right to be." She let me smooth the hair off her face, but she wouldn't look at me directly. "He lied to you and it hurts. But I think part of this is you being scared that he's sick."

"Of course I'm scared..." She closed her eyes as a new torrent of tears started down her face. Then, as if something had just occurred to her, Sammy smacked my arm, pushing me away from her. "Where the hell have you been all week? You just disappear on me? I needed you, and you just leave me alone?"

Scrubbing my face, I took a minute, not real sure how to play this. I didn't want to hand her a line of bullshit and I didn't want her mad, but she needed me. She needed someone, even if she'd never ask for help. "I...thought it would be better if I gave you some space. Liam Shane is..."

"I swear to God, Johnny Carelli, if you hand me some bullshit line about protecting me...""It's not a line," I said, my own anger mounting. "Besides, I heard you and Indra talking. You were miserable. I was making you miserable. I just want you to be happy."

"You know what would make me happy?" She pushed me again, her cheeks flaming red. "If all the damn men in my life would give me credit enough to protect myself!"

She started to walk away, taking quick steps backward, but I held her, taking her arm, desperate not to let her leave. Not like this. Not if I could help her. "Please," I told her, curling my arms around her shoulders, twisting my fingers in her hair. "I just want to make sure you're safe and happy. That's all I've ever wanted."

"That's not your job, Johnny," she said, her voice flat, still angry.

She let me dry her face, holding her still with my thumb against her cheek, my mouth on her forehead. "I want it to be. Still. Always, *bella*. That's all I'll ever want."

"You want to help me?" Her voice came out higher, and Sammy stifled the sob that got stuck in her throat.

"I'd do anything for you. You know that."

It was a long two seconds while she watched me, her expression blank, her eyes widening as though she debated something she would keep to herself. Finally, the green of her eyes darkened, and Sammy shook her head, tightening her mouth until it resembled a hard line.

"Then take off your clothes and get on your back."

Sammy had never made any demands of me. She took my body when she wanted it, but never first, never without me encouraging her. And it had always come from somewhere warm. There was nothing like that in her expression. She was still angry. Still hurt and scared. But if she needed this from me, it was what she'd get.

The only consent I gave her was the slow nod of my head before I stepped away, already untucking my shirt to unbutton it as she leaned on my desk. Sammy's expression stayed neutral, didn't change at all until I slipped out of my shoes and loosened my belt, unbuckling and lowering the zipper on my pants. Then, her gaze was on me, and her attention was enough to turn me on.

She took two steps, her gaze roaming over my chest, not touching me as I stood there, watching her untie the straps of her sundress and slide the light fabric off her body.

"Lie down," she said, her voice low, hungry. She nodded to the floor, and I obeyed, loving how she owned me, wanting her to touch me, wanting her mouth on me.

Sammy slipped out of her sandals and pulled down her thong, crawling on top of me. Her mouth glided up my thigh, licking and teasing, cupping me, tasting just the tip of me until I was wet enough, ready enough, and she put my cock inside her, guiding me with her strong, sure fingers.

"*Bella*...oh Christ..."

That earned me a glare as she tortured me, but I didn't care. She felt too good all over me, tightening, clamping down on me... It was all I could do to just hang on, let her use me, abuse me, however she wanted.

"Anything...anything...I...want..." she said. Her movements were sloppy, disjointed, the harder she rode me.

I arched up, steadying her, and the light coming from the desk lamp hit her face. I stopped moving altogether, seeing the heavy tears and the anguish twisting her features. "Sammy..." I said, holding her as she fell against my chest. "*Amore mia* ...please..."

"It's all a lie..."

"I'm not lying," I told her, lifting her head to look in her eyes. "I'd never lie to you."

She closed her eyes, mumbling something I couldn't hear under her breath. I wanted to understand, wanted her to tell me what she needed from me, but her cell rang. Sammy moved, sliding off me to grab her phone.

I sat there, wondering how much more of a mess we could make of our lives when I heard her answer the call.

"Yes, this is she. Okay...is he speaking?" She exhaled.

I watched her in the reflection in the window, spotting the relief I knew she'd never let me see if she knew I was looking.

"I'll be there in twenty minutes."

She hung up, hurrying around my office to dress, and I followed her lead. I pulled on my shorts and pants, not bothering with my shirt. I knew her well enough to know she wouldn't want a chaperone to confront her uncle. "I'm glad he's okay."

She nodded, not looking at me.

I knew none of the problems we'd had before she walked into this office had been settled.

"Sammy..."

"You did lie," she said, cutting me off as she pulled back her hair and twisted it into a messy knot. "You lied then. You lied about what my uncle said to you in his office." She turned, finally facing me. "Men lie. I get that now. Even very good men." I stepped toward her, meaning to stop her when she started for the door. "Don't worry about it, Johnny. I can handle things myself."

Sammy left before I could catch her. I swore I heard her mumble something that made no sense to me then. Something that would haunt me until I was hunting her down, desperate to find out what had happened to her.

It came out as an afterthought, a throwaway statement she likely didn't think I heard; something that stung more than anything she'd ever said to me before.

"We don't need you."

Chapter Seventeen
Sammy

Patrick's breaths were even, and the monitor next to his bed marked a lowering temperature and blood pressure level.

He was cooling, his skin no longer blazing-hot.

He was calm now, healing.

I wasn't faring as well.

"He's in and out," the nurse said, getting a nod from me.

I kept my attention on the man in the bed. The woman fiddled with the machine, checking tubes and medicine, while I could only watch and wait.

I'd taken my time getting back to the hospital. I wasn't eager to face him or confront all the lies he'd constructed for the past thirty years. There were so many questions. So many things that made no sense to me. So many facts hidden behind cover-ups and half-truths. My apartment was closer to the hospital than the rectory, but after I'd stopped home for a change of clothes, I'd gone by my uncle's place to grab evidence. He'd wake up and I'd say my piece. After that, I had no idea what would happen.

The picture in my hand seemed like such a monumental thing, volatile like a grenade with the pin already pulled. It rested on my lap, my parents' smiling faces staring back at me—one dead now, one likely dying on the bed in front of me.

"Samantha?" he said, his voice weak and breathy. I didn't take his hand when he reached for me, and he noticed, leaning in my direction, a frown already forming on his face. "What is it, sweetheart?"

He followed me with his gaze as I moved from my chair to his side next to the bed, silent, my expression neutral. There was nothing I could say that would make a bigger impact than the picture in my hand, so I handed it over, placing it on his chest, my attention never leaving his face as he picked it up.

The confusion that made him look so much older when he woke shifted instantly as his gaze lowered and he moved his eyes down to the photo, looking at the image of a thirty-years-younger version of himself and the woman he claimed to love holding their baby.

I wondered how long he considered lying. I wondered if he had a blanket explanation cued up should anyone, especially me, ever come across this picture and connect the dots like I had. But as he went on looking at that picture, as the years seemed to flit through his mind the longer he stared at my mother's beautiful face, clarity and surrender seemed to crash together, and Patrick—my uncle? my father?—decided not to bother with a lie.

"Does anyone else know?" he asked, wincing when I laughed. "I don't mean to sound indelicate, but there is a protocol. It's the only reason I ask."

"There's a protocol?"

He stared into the hallway, looking very old and very tired as two nurses passed by. Patrick leaned back, moving the picture to the tray at his side. "Bishop Williamson stipulated that you were to be cared for when he placed me here. We weren't to be transferred for any reason. It was unspoken. He prepared the necessary paperwork, had you and Ava made legal, but officially, he knew nothing. He was a good man and understood...how mistakes can be made." He closed his eyes, hands rubbing into his lids before he looked at me again. "He let me go on telling the story of her being rejected by her husband. He believed I would be a good priest. And when she died..." He crossed himself, suddenly overcome with emotion, tears dotting his lashes. "This isn't Ireland, mind. The Church here hasn't begun to acknowledge children fathered by priests, and we knew that. You were allowed to live at the school as a ward because you were my family.

"But if anyone ever discovered the truth, the Bishop made me promise I would leave the Church and absolve him of any knowledge." Patrick rubbed his face, letting his head fall back against his pillow.

"Bishop Williamson died fifteen years ago," I said, not understanding why he was so upset.

"It would tarnish his memory and his reputation if anyone knew what he permitted." He lifted his head to look again at the picture but didn't touch it. The old priest glanced at me, looking like he wanted to say something, but instead, kept silent. "Did you tell anyone?"

I said nothing, but I watched him, letting him guess.

He knew me well enough to know whom I'd run to and why I'd done it. Patrick let his head fall back against the pillow, and he looked up at the ceiling, eyes wide. "That boy..."

"Is no different from you."

He jerked his gaze to me, face pinking. "I am nothing like..."

"Johnny fell in love with a girl who was off-limits... like you." Patrick looked away from me, staring again at the ceiling. "He got that girl pregnant but couldn't marry her...like you." I stood, leaning against the cabinet behind me, watching the man I'd known as my uncle shake his head and mutter under his breath, small prayers I doubted anyone would answer. "And like you, a stubborn old priest kept Johnny swimming in shame and resentment until it nearly undid him."

"I have paid my penance for my sin…"

"That's what I am to you?" I asked him, not surprised when he refused to look at me. "I read your letters. A long time ago, you claimed to love her."

"I *do* love her." For the first time, he showed real emotion. His voice cracked, and there was a shake in his hand when he reached for me.

But I didn't touch him. I couldn't. "But you can't see how Johnny loves me, or why I'd want Betta to know her father? When you spent my entire life keeping me from the truth? You want me to keep my daughter from the truth too?"

"Don't you see? The mistakes we made… I broke my vow, and it cost me…her. God took her from me because I disobeyed Him." He sat up, tears on his face now. "And you made the same mistake. The very same. I could not let you die too, not you or that beautiful baby…"

"But you wanted me to marry him!"

"*That* was a mistake," he said, closing his eyes. "It was rash, and I thank God above the boy refused. God knows what would have happened to you and the baby if you'd married that boy or what He would have done in punishment for your sin! Just like my beloved Ava."

"God didn't kill my mother," I told him. "He doesn't kill innocent people."

"Samantha…" he tried, leaning against the railing on the bed when I grabbed my bag and made for the door. "Please, child. I have made mistakes, but that boy…"

"That boy is none of your business anymore," I told him, turning back to take my mother's picture off the tray. "None of us are."

Chapter Eighteen
Johnny

There had been only one message. An image. That beautiful face—the high cheekbones, the pouting, arched mouth. The stuff of every fantasy I'd had since I was eighteen.

Streaks of black down her cheeks.

Smudged makeup.

Green, green eyes clouded with fear, soaking in tears.

Three words and my life changed forever.

Come find us.

That motherfucker had no idea what he asked for.

Chapter Nineteen
Johnny

The hospital staff knew me. Dr. Matthews had been Chief of Staff when my father got his diagnosis, and we'd paid a lot of money to make sure that stayed out of the papers. This would too. Angelo sent Sal, his nephew, to make that assurance.

"Tell your men, no one goes in or out."

"And if the old man gives us grief?" This kid, Matteo, I think his name was, was new, another one of Angelo's men brought in from Newark.

"He won't," I told him, staring at the door that led to Father Patrick's room, "I'm about to handle that."

Angelo stepped up to me, leaning down to catch my ear before I opened the door. "Should we be bothering with this old asshole? He hates you, man, and Smoke and Dario have already left..."

"If anything happens to him, no matter how pissed off she is, Sammy will never recover. If I have the chance to keep him safe, I'll do it." Angelo nodded, grabbing the door for me so I could walk inside.

The priest lay sleeping, his head moving restlessly on the pillow as the night nurse I hired two hours ago watched his vitals. She had dark skin and black eyes, was curvy but cut and wore black scrubs, her hair pulled back. She was more polished and professional than the hospital staff, for good reason. Private care nurses like her came with stealthier training and protection you couldn't learn in nursing school. It was the reason there was a nine strapped to her ankle and two blades concealed at her waist.

"We good?" I asked her, watching the old man mutter under his breath.

"He's got a fever, and it's spiking. It's not surprising, given his age and the stress he's under. The doctor will be back after his shift, but for now, I'm monitoring him."

"Unless he codes..."

"I understand, Mr. Carelli. No one in or out." She adjusted his IV once more, flicking the drip before she nodded to me. "I'll give you a moment."

When the nurse left the room, I stood there watching the old man, wondering if he could hear me. But I instantly corrected myself. If Patrick Nicola had any idea I stood this close to him, he'd be using the last stores of his health to curse my immortal soul just for daring to breathe the same air as him.

"You are a piece of work, you know that, old man?" I told him, wondering if he'd ever understand how much Sammy had cried for him or how much she'd suffered because men like us couldn't stop lying to her.

I turned, readying to get out of this place and find Liam, to get Sammy away from him, when Patrick made a sound, the low moan of a delirious man, crying out from pain or sickness. "Not...yours..." he said, his voice clearing as I faced him. He kept his eyes closed, but he'd tightened his fingers around the railing. "You can't have them...my girls..."

"I only want Sammy," I told him, head shaking with pity at how out of his head the priest had become.

"She doesn't want you," he wheezed. Those blue eyes were hazy, moving around the room as though he couldn't find a single thing to focus on. "Samantha... she wants...her...just Betta..."

"She'll have better..."

"Idiot boy..." he said, swiping at the air like I was a bug he couldn't kill. "Her child... Betta..." Patrick inhaled, the explanation coming out in a rushing breath that had me staggering back, falling against the wall. "Sammy's child, Elizabetta. She...only wants to keep her from you."

"That's not..."

That name... Sammy knew what it meant. Why it was important.

The room seemed to pulse and bend around me. My head swam, and I couldn't decide if the old man was delirious and fabricating impossible scenarios, or if the person I loved most in the world had lied to me.

The rush of possibility was too much.

He couldn't be serious.

He was high, not thinking clearly.

Sammy never had...

But I wouldn't know, would I?

I left her.

I broke her heart and didn't see her for a year.

Then I broke her heart again and didn't see her for nine more years after that.

A sick, bitter taste filled my mouth, and I thought I might vomit.

Patrick fell back against the pillow, finally passing out, his grip on the railing loosening just as the private nurse entered the room. "Mr. Carelli?"

I lifted my hand, quieting her, unable to speak at all. I kept that hand raised until I moved out of the room and found Angelo, calling him over, still so rattled by the possibility of that delusional man's words that I had to lean against the wall to steady myself.

But there were too many eyes on me. Too much attention on everything I did. This wasn't the time or place to lose it. There was a plan in play, and I had to execute it.

Sammy needed me.

"I got a job only you can do," I told Angelo, pressing one hand on the wall as I looked down at the floor, watching my feet as I spoke. The sick feeling wouldn't leave me. Angelo was at my side, nodding, and I caught his profile in the corner of my eye as he scanned the hallway, gaze focused on the guards around us. "Get to Sammy's building. Night guard likes the ponies. Tell him about the race next weekend and that jockey with the smack problem. It's an easy win if he bets against him. And slip him two large to get into her apartment." Angelo glanced at me, a question in that expression he needed answered. "I want to know who else lives there. I need pictures of the second bedroom and anything that might clue you in to who that person is." Angelo gave me another nod, starting to walk down the hall, but he stopped when I tugged him back by the collar.

"If this person is who the old man says they are, then we got someone else to protect, and I'm gonna need all the information on them." I touched his chest, driving home my point. "No one is more important to me now, you feel me?"

"I feel you, boss," Angelo said, his face serious. He gave me a tap on the shoulder, and then he was gone.

"Sal," I called, wiping my mouth, and the boy was at my side before Angelo had made it down the hallway. "Get the car." I pulled out my cell and texted my cousin as the kid jogged next to me toward the stairs. "We got somewhere to be."

Chapter Twenty
Johnny

The Suburban was parked two blocks from the warehouse, four car lengths behind a busted yellow bus that had seen better days. Much like the Suburban. Had to hand it to my cousins; they had paid attention when I'd schooled them on going incognito. They had it down to an art form.

Two knocks on the window and the locks disengaged. I slipped inside alone, nodding to Dario and Smoke, my eyebrows shooting up when I spotted the youngest of my uncle Sonny's sons, Dante, in the middle of the middle row.

Despite my worry and the shock of everything I'd just discovered, seeing the skinny kid I'd always known grown into a massive man built like a stone wall knocked me out of my foul mood.

"Fuck me, bean pole," I greeted, unable to keep from smiling at the kid's sheer size. "What kind of grapes they got at that vineyard?"

"Fat ones," he said, offering me his hand to shake.

I took it, slapping his shoulder once before looking over to his brothers, the small laughter at seeing my cousin leaving me when I spotted the warehouse.

She was in there.

Alone with that fucker.

I could kill him with my bare hands.

"We confirmed he's in there?" I asked, eager to pounce, to do something that got me my hands around Shane's fucking neck.

"He's there. Ralphie checked. Besides, that asshole Liam used this place to cook meth," Dante said, dropping his eyes to stare at his fingers. It was shit he'd been involved in that had landed Dario in prison, and I guessed Liam was the source of that shit.

"You steal his money?" I asked him, moving a hand to the back of my little cousin's neck. Not to threaten him so much as to make sure he gave me an honest answer. "That why my woman got tied up in this shit?"

"I took his money, true enough. But hell, man, that was five years ago." He was man enough to look at me, eyes clear, expression sorry. His size didn't worry me. He could be seven feet tall and weigh the same as a Volkswagen. To me, he was still my punk little cousin. Dante frowned, I guessed not liking the look I shot his way. "But from what I've heard, it ain't about the money anymore." He flashed his phone at me, his thumb scrolling over a series of text messages. "This dumbass is complaining about being disrespected in front of a bunch of kids and your girl. I think he wants you to think he can't be handled like that, and from what he's been telling people, he wants the girl. He's so full of himself because he knows we're coming."

Smoke shook his head. I caught the movement in my peripheral, but Dante missed his slipup. It was instinctual, me squeezing his neck, just a small correction I needed to impart. "That's no girl," I told him, voice low but calm. "That is a woman."

He winced, moving away from my grip. "Got it. She's a woman. Man, I didn't..."

"I told you," Smoke said, staring at his little brother in the rearview, "it's gonna take more than pruning vines and weeding plants to make up for the shitty mess you made." He nodded to me, and I moved my hand off the kid's neck. "We have two men on the roof across from the warehouse. Ralphie is about to check in."

The Suburban went silent, except for the vibration of Dante's phone, until my own phone chirped, the movement of the alert pulsating in my pocket. I pulled it out, sliding open the message alert. I saw Angelo's name, his text making the breath freeze somewhere in the center of my chest.

Gotta be yours, boss. Got your mouth. Your cheeks. Looks just like Cara did when she was little. 'Cept the eyes.

He wasn't wrong. Those were Sammy's eyes staring back at me from the picture Angelo had sent along. Older pictures of her as a baby, of Sammy holding an infant that looked exactly like me. The little girl—Elizabetta, Patrick had called her—and the priest at her birthday party, years and years of memories all on display in a purple and green room decorated with dragons and unicorns, filled with books and pictures along bookshelves and tables.

I'd missed this that night at Sammy's. I'd been so focused on her, on being with her, that I hadn't bothered to look around and see what her life looked like.

The life she led with my daughter.

Our daughter.

"Heads up. We got eyes on them," Smoke said, killing the engine. "That dumb asshole only has six guards with him. Three in back, three in front. Let's get it."

The street was quiet, with only a few stragglers walking away from the warehouse. None of them were paying attention to the six men trailing down the sidewalk and weaving around the parked cars to get to the side entrances. My cousins and I moved to the front, while Sal and Matteo took the rear.

I couldn't shake the worry and the anger I felt. They spread inside me like a virus. I wasn't sure where it came from. Equal parts of me wanted to scream at Sammy. I wanted her to hurt as badly as I did. I wanted to see her cry and wail. Some sick part thought she deserved this shit laid at her feet right now for keeping me from my child.

I pushed that stupidity away, knowing the anger had no place in my brain. Not when I needed to be on guard. Not when Liam fucking Shane deserved all my rage.

If he hurt her, I swear to Christ...

"I got four guys on each side," Smoke said, pulling my attention from the bullshit in my head. He impressed me with how prepared he came with little notice. "What's that face?" We hunched down near the entrance, guns drawn and cocked, waiting on Ralphie's signal.

"You're not exactly *in the family,* and you're locked and ready to go like this? Took me a few hours to get my crew together when that shit went down with Cara and Kiel."

"You gotta streamline, cousin," Smoke said, winking at me. "Keep a small but effective crew." His smile lowered when I only nodded, too distracted to give more than a passing notice of his joke. Smoke was smart and probably more perceptive than anybody I knew. My bet was that he got what this did to me, not knowing where Sammy was or what Liam had done to her. But he couldn't know what was going on in my head. "We'll get her," he said, nudging my shoulder. When I glanced at him, nodding, my cousin gripped my arm, crouching in front of me. He stared hard, removing anything but sincerity from his expression. "We got you, man, and we got her. Don't doubt that."

"I know." He watched me, likely wanting to make sure I understood him, then we both looked up, staring in the direction of the whistle that came from the roof across the street.

"Movement inside," Smoke said, nodding for his brothers and his crew to take position.

My heart thumped hard. I shut my eyes, pulling in a few quick breaths, muttering quicker prayers that she was safe, that I could get to her before Liam did anything she couldn't walk away from...that the asshole would know a special kind of pain for even thinking he could take her in the first place. And then...we moved.

There was an incline at the front of the building, and we made our way up it. Smoke and Dario were behind me, Dante pulling up the rear. To my left, I heard the low rumble of bodies falling as my cousin's and my men tussled with whoever was Liam's lookout, and then we emerged through the large loading dock at the front.

Two massive doors were unlocked and open, and over the racket of fighting and the smattering of gunshots, I made out a woman's shout. My heartbeat hammered faster than a hummingbird's wings now, and I edged farther ahead of my cousins as we came to a stack of crates and the screaming voice I heard turned into words. Sammy was fighting, and the sound of it twisted something inside me.

"No, you son of a bitch, get off me!" Her voice carried over the noise around us, echoing in the nearly empty warehouse. There was the thunder of running feet and falling bodies, the still zipping buzz of bullets flying, and then, a loud, crashing thud. Her yell lifted, piercingly loud, but I couldn't make out much in the darkness.

"Stupid, no-good..."

"Sammy?" I shouted, stopping short when she came around the largest stack of crates, carrying a crowbar in her right hand.

"Johnny?" She stopped short, eyes fluttering as she stood near a broken window above, a sliver of moonlight coming down to illuminate the small section of warehouse like light from a prism. Mouth dropping open, like she wasn't sure she was really seeing me, Sammy shot her gaze to my face, then around to my cousins, before she lowered her shoulders, dropped the metal with a clatter against the floor, and ran straight for me. "Oh God!"

"It's okay..." I soothed, curling her against my chest. "I've got you, *bella*..." My anger at her evaporated, and the beat of my heart quickened for a different reason.

I'd never felt such relief.

I'd never been so grateful.

A quick glance at my cousins and a nod in the direction Sammy had come from, and Dante and Dario ran farther into the warehouse as Smoke stepped back, pulling out his phone to tell our men to stand down.

"Johnny...I'm sorry," she said, fingers curling into my shirt. "About how I left...how I acted...I was mad... and hurt..."

"Shh, hush, *cuore mia*. It doesn't matter." I kissed the top of her head, inhaling that rich, sweet scent before I angled her face up, my blood burning when I spotted the cut along her jaw and the bruise under her eye.

"It's fine," she told me, pulling my fingers away from her bruises. "He kept waving that stupid crowbar at me, and when he heard your men, he got all excited. Kept bragging about how he was going to take you out." She shook her head, wiping the moisture and grime from her forehead. "He was distracted, so I grabbed the bar and knocked him across the back of the head." Sammy turned, frowning. "I know it's not... very Christian of me to say, but..."

"It's okay to want that bastard to bleed," I told her, unable to keep from holding her close. When Dante and Dario came back into sight, Sammy stiffened in my arms, her eyes widening as my cousins shrugged, coming back without Liam.

"But he was right there," she promised, looking between us.

"It's okay, *bella*," I promised her. She took the kiss I gave her, relaxing a little. "We'll find him." To my cousins, I nodded when they left the warehouse. "Let's go," I told Sammy, leading her toward the door, but she stopped me, tugging on my hand.

"Johnny...there's something..."

"I know there is." She frowned, her expression tensing when I dropped her hand. "There's a lot we've got to say." I glanced up, just noticing the burned scent in the warehouse, some remnant of the lab Liam had held here. My temper rose, knowing Sammy had been inside this place, inhaling all this shit. I wanted her out of there. "But not here," I told her, nodding toward the door. "Come on. Let me take you home."

Chapter Twenty-One
Johnny

Mina's smile dropped when I ushered Sammy through the door.

"Ah!" the housekeeper cried, instantly glaring at me. "What did you do?"

"Wasn't me." The old woman took Sammy from me with little argument and led her to my master bath. "That cut on her jaw," I said, tugging off my jacket and shoes as Mina settled a fussing Sammy on the closed toilet. "Stitches, you think?"

"I'm fine," Sammy argued, her voice kind but insistent. "Mina, please..."

"Samantha Nicola, what would your uncle say if he knew I didn't patch you up right?"

I glanced at Sammy when she looked up, deciding it was pointless to correct my housekeeper about the priest's relationship to Sammy. No one knew, from what she'd told me on the ride back to my apartment. And as far as she was concerned, no one would find out anytime soon. "If he wants to keep me as his dirty secret, then let him," she'd said, curled up against the car door, rubbing her temples like it would help keep the raging headache she complained about at bay.

"He's in the hospital," Sammy admitted, making Mina pause to look at her.

"Oh no." Mina moved to sit on the edge of the tub, a cotton swab dipped in alcohol held between her fingers. "Is he going to be…"

"It was a heart attack. I don't know how he is." That came out sharply, and Sammy must have heard the tone in her own voice or seen Mina's quick reaction. She sat up, grabbing the woman's hand, holding it in between both of hers. "I'm so tired, Mina, and my head is pounding. I'll wash my face, and maybe you can call Dr. Michaels for me in an hour to see about those stitches. In the meantime, would you mind saying a prayer for my uncle?"

Mina's expression shifted, and the change was immediate—the quick surprise moving into a smile as she patted Sammy's cheek and kissed her forehead. "Of course, *piccola*. Of course I will. You clean up and rest. Johnny will get you an aspirin from his medicine cabinet and let you have his bed, I'm sure." She shot me a glance, smiling when I nodded. "I'll be back with the doctor soon."

I helped Mina stand, taking the cotton swabs from her, and let her kiss my cheek before she left the room. Sammy watched her, watched how she doted on me. It was normal for me to have the woman look after me and the people I cared for. Sammy hadn't had that, I realized.

Still, that was no excuse.

"She's a good woman," Sammy said, watching me as I pulled out two aspirin from the bottle and filled a glass with tap water. She took the pills, nodding a thanks, and continued to follow my movements as I took a clean washcloth from the cabinet and ran the hot water. I gave her a smile, then pointed to the free space on the counter, reaching for the antibiotic wash as she sat next to the sink. "She's always taken good care of you. Just like Marcella."

"They've both been loyal," I agreed, squeezing out the rag and setting it on the side of the faucet. Marcella had been Mina's mother and had raised both Cara and me after our mother's death. My father had always kept a devoted staff who were more family than employees.

"Loyalty is important," Sammy said, looking up at me when I stood between her legs, my hands lathered with soap, ready to rub away the grime from her face.

Shifting my gaze to hers, I arched my eyebrows, knowing she understood me, knowing we weren't just talking about good employees now. "Loyalty is everything."

She leaned into my touch, holding her hair back from her face, eyes closing, her full, tempting lips plump, ready for me to take. I wouldn't. Not when I didn't know what would come out of them. Lies? Half-truths? Bullshit she made up to keep me in the dark? All the things she thought I wanted to hear?

"Here," I said, grabbing the rag, deciding she could handle rinsing her own face clean as I walked into my room before I touched her, before I got so angry my shouts rattled the windows. "You'll probably want a bath." She opened her mouth, but I didn't let her speak, moving quickly to turn on the tap for the tub, jerking open the cabinet to grab fresh towels for her before I left, closing the door behind me.

Twenty minutes later, Sammy emerged from my bathroom sporting my robe, smelling of my soap with her hair wet and her skin scrubbed clean.

"Johnny?" she called, holding her cell between her fingers as she found me in an armchair next to my window.

I didn't look at her, letting my own cell sit loosely in my hand as I scrolled through the images Angelo had sent me, one beautiful picture of my daughter after another. Each one chiseling away another piece of my heart.

"Your uncle did a shitty thing to you," I said, not looking at her as she sat on the end of my bed. My attention was focused on that beautiful face, those green eyes like her mother's and a face so like the one

I'd seen in the mirror every day of my life. "All those years, lying to you, keeping you in the dark."

"It...it *was* a...shitty thing to do."

"So, why then, Samantha, haven't you told me, nine years later, about my daughter?" I looked at her, noticed how she opened her mouth, her surprise turning her cheeks pink before I tossed my phone to her.

She caught it, attention shooting to the screen, thumb moving through each picture before she lowered her hand, resting the phone in her lap. It took her several seconds before she seemed able to look at me. And when she did, her eyes had darkened and were shining.

"Johnny..."

"Where is she?"

Her breathing quickened, like she wasn't sure if answering me would seal a fate she wanted. But then Sammy nodded, her shoulders lowering, and the tears fell. "In Ellenville at summer camp. She's safe. We made sure...she's safe."

"You weren't tonight."

"*She* is," Sammy said, wiping her hand across her cheek. "Uncle...Pat. He had the place investigated." When I frowned, Sammy shrugged as though I should know better than to wonder how a priest could have access to that kind of security. "He takes Betta's safety seriously. More so than anyone else's."

"Because she's yours?"

She sighed, her mouth tightening. "Because she's yours, Johnny."

I wanted her to shut up.

I wanted her to apologize.

I wanted to hate her.

I wanted to kiss her.

I wanted her to disappear.

I wanted her to tell me every detail of my child's life.

I wanted her to beg for my forgiveness.

I wanted to bury myself inside her.

I wanted her to never touch me again.

Instead, I dropped my head, my throat locking up, face falling into my hands as I tried to hide myself from her, from the world, from the jumble of thoughts I had at that very moment.

Sammy came to me slowly. Her movements quiet, her touch soundless. I only felt the brush of her fingers against my leg as she knelt in front of me, then her palms on my thighs as she moved closer.

"Sammy..." I warned, not knowing what I wanted from her.

Her scent came to me like a whisper until the only thing I knew was her arms around me and her mouth against my forehead.

"It was...the only way," she said, and I hated the truth in each word. "Your family...the life you live, Johnny... I couldn't..." She went quiet when I touched her, grabbing her arm to pull her closer.

Sammy knew something I'd never been able to admit out loud. The same reason I couldn't marry her when I was a kid, no matter how much I may have wanted to. The reason I was willing to destroy her at eighteen. My family could get her killed. It had gotten two innocent boys killed, and they weren't even related to my family. It had taken years for my father to recover from that guilt and to begin the hard task of working toward legitimacy, something I was still trying to do. Hell, Sammy could have died tonight. We'd been lucky. Shane was an idiot. He had zero clout. But Vinnie hadn't been like Liam Shane. He'd nearly killed my sister and brother-in-law.

If it hadn't been for Kiel's family, I might not have my sister.

"I'm sorry," she said, holding me tight, arms locked around me like she had no plans to ever let me go. "I had to protect her."

"I...I know that," I finally said, pushing her away. My face was wet, my eyes swollen as I looked at her. "But my God, *bella,* this hurts. I...I would have found a way."

"It doesn't matter, not anymore." Sammy held my face, kissing me, her own tears wetting my cheeks. "I'm so sorry I kept her away. I'm so sorry you didn't know about her... She's so..." Her smile was infectious, growing wider when she opened the gallery on her phone. "She's so smart and brave and, *oh God,* Johnny, she has the best laugh... She has your laugh and...and...look..."

There were so many pictures—hundreds, so many of our daughter laughing and playing, being silly, dancing with her friends, playing volleyball. And videos, so many videos of her singing and sleeping, at the zoo with Sammy, riding an elephant, on a farm upstate feeding baby goats from a bottle. My heart swelled, and I took her phone, pulling Sammy onto my lap as we both looked at our daughter, at all the times and places I'd missed.

"What did you name her?" I asked, already knowing part of the answer as my thumb worked overtime to move through each image. I was greedy for every picture, each detail that would fill in the spaces I'd never known.

"Elizabetta," she said, curling her arm around my shoulder as we looked at the pictures. "You told me once it was..."

"My mother's middle name. Yeah, *bella*, it was." I squeezed her, kissing her cheek. *"Grazie."*

"Elizabetta Roseline. That was my mother's middle name."

"It's beautiful," I told her, setting the phone on the table at my side. *"She's* beautiful." Sammy watched me, her eyes unblinking as I reached for her, shifting her head closer. "Whatever it takes, I'll do it. I'll walk away from this life. I'll give up every penny I have. I want her. I want you. I want our family. I want to meet her... When can I..."

"Soon... Next week, she comes home. But, Johnny..."

"Please, Sammy, you're here. You're safe." I felt a little punch-drunk and desperate, wanting so much to make up for what had been taken from me. I wanted everything to settle and sort until I had them both with me, together. Until we could eliminate the distance, the separation, and get on with the business of living our lives together.

"My daughter is safe. And next week, she will know me. Everything else will work itself out."

"Johnny...this will be complicated...all of this..."

"Nothing is complicated about this, *bella*," I said, kissing her silent. She moved against me, her body relaxing into mine when she wrapped her legs around my waist. "This, you and me, everything that happens from now on, this was the dream. It starts now."

"What about..."

I didn't let her lay question after question in our way. I lifted Sammy from the chair, carrying her against me to my bed, stealing her breath with every kiss until she relaxed, until she let me slide over her, my mouth on her neck, moving lower, my tongue gliding across all the skin I uncovered when I untied my robe and found her naked underneath.

"Every time I see you like this," I told her, my fingers curling around her hips, "I'm a kid again, crazed with lust, fully possessed at just the sight of you." I moved down, adjusting her on the bed, pulling her closer, stroking my hands over her ribs to cradle her generous breasts. "I could kiss you here," I said, placing one reverent kiss over her nipple, holding it against my mouth. "And here." Another across her hip, my free hand cupping the round curve of her thigh. "And I'd never be full."

"Johnny..." she whined. My name left her mouth like a prayer, and her hands greedily tugged at the blankets when I kissed her full on her pussy. "Ah... *oddio...*"

Then I stopped talking, diving into her. My tongue and mouth working, caressing. My hands under her ass, pressing her to my lips as I sucked her. Sammy wrapped her legs around my head and gripped my hair, riding my face, the sensation between us seeming to drive her over the edge as I teased and tasted her. So fucking sweet. So delicious. My *bella* Sammy. And when I fingered her, using my index and thumb inside her pussy and against her ass, she arched, her screams loud, her heels on my shoulders as she flooded my mouth with her orgasm.

"God...oh God..." she cried, breathless, overwhelmed as she fell back against the mattress, pulling on me, tugging me close as I hurried to free my cock and get inside her.

She reached for me, greedy grabs around my waist, down the front of my cock. I had to hold her wrist, twist my head away against the sensation of how good her fingers and hand felt on me.

"*Bella*...shit..."

"I need you. Please, Johnny...I need you inside me."

Fuck me, that's all I'd ever wanted to hear from her.

She opened for me, knees wide, ready as I held myself to her. She took me as I entered, both of us gasping, the contact like coming home, filling up the silence with sound and light and impossible sensation. I knew this was where I belonged—in this heat, surrounded by all this perfection, feeling needed, feeling full. Only Sammy gave me that. Only I could give that to her.

I rocked into her, her tight walls clamping down, my bed shifting as I leaned over her, going deep, shuddering when she grabbed my ass, pushing me closer and closer inside her.

"Johnny... *please,* I need...everything..."

And I gave it to her...for hours or years until we both went boneless.

The sheets twisted around us like vines clinging to our sweaty skin, but the only sensation I felt was the slight weight of Sammy's body on my chest and the tickle of her hair against my arms.

We didn't sleep.

We'd fucked and napped and bathed.

We'd sent Mina and the doctor away, ignored her knock for food and every call that came to us. There would be time for everything. For now, there was just the two of us.

Sammy yawned against my nipple, the slow, smooth tease of her fingernail along my chest making me sleepy, but I couldn't think of anything. Nothing but the question and her answer and what she would say. I'd practiced it a thousand times. How to phrase it, how to sound like a tough guy doing it, how not to embarrass myself. But when the time came, it was quiet and simple and nothing like I'd imagined.

"Sammy?" I said, getting a low, sleepy sound from her as acknowledgment before I swallowed and let the words spill out. "Marry me, *si?*"

The slow stroke of her finger paused, the nail pointing into my skin for two full seconds before she rested her palm against my chest and I felt the stretch of her mouth pressing into my skin. "Okay, Johnny," she said before she returned to the gentle movement of her finger trailing over my chest.

Chapter Twenty-Two
Sammy

"Are you sure he likes chicken Marsala?" Betta lifted the lid on the pan and sniffed. She squinted her eyes like there was some alien life-form in that pan and not the meal I'd been working on all afternoon.

"You act like I've never cooked before." When I slapped her hand away from the lid, my daughter wrinkled her nose, still not convinced. "And yes, it's his favorite. I'm even using his housekeeper's recipe."

"Is he fat?"

"He's not remotely fat, Betta."

She'd began the third degree the second I picked her up from camp and we'd stopped at the small diner just outside of the city for a late breakfast. It was a summer tradition, and I used that meal as the

229

opportunity to tell her about Pat's heart attack *and* her father.

It could have gone better.

"Where's he been my whole life?"

That was a problem Johnny and I had argued about for an entire week—we both wanted to take the blame. We settled on vagueness. Nine was too young to tell Betta about her father's business, and we hoped by the time she was old enough, that business wouldn't be a consideration.

"Set the table, please," I told her when my "not fat" comment didn't seem to convince her.

"I'm just saying, there's a lot of calories in that stuff."

"Says the girl who downs cheese sticks and Sour Patch Kids like water."

"And," she continued, choosing to ignore my dig, "I don't think it's fair to the chicken..."

I moved out of the kitchen, still holding three glasses in my hand. "Are you telling me you're a vegetarian now?"

She looked at me, narrowed eyes serious, like she needed a second to consider her answer before she shrugged. "The trout situation really made me think."

I nodded, not buying it. "Hmm...well, that would mean you'd have to avoid Sister Dominique's thick-crust chicken tenders during the holidays..." Out of the corner of my eye, I caught the wince Betta tried to hide, but I didn't call her on it. When she flopped into a chair, I sat next to her, placing the glasses in the empty space in front of me. "You don't have to eat the Marsala. I made a salad too."

"It's fine," she said, pouting.

"And mashed potatoes." A shrug this time and now she didn't bother to look at me. "Do you think maybe you're still a little irritated about Uncle..."

"Grandpa?"

"Patrick?" She looked at me, her expression set hard, but she didn't respond. "Whatever he may have told you about your father, you have to know, it was only his opinion." Betta fiddled with a butter knife, rubbing the tip against the tablecloth. "If Johnny had known about you, he would have been there.""Then you should have told him," she said, her voice sharp. When I tilted my head, understanding the attitude but not appreciating the tone, she deflated. "Why didn't you?"

"It...wasn't—" The knock on the door interrupted me, and we both bolted from the table. The sound transformed Betta's attitude, and she instantly straightened, pulling down her dress, adjusting the collar. I shot a glance at her, hoping the smile I gave her relaxed her before I squeezed her hand and headed for the door. "It's okay," I whispered to her, winking before I opened it.

"Bella," Johnny greeted, stepping into the apartment, his hands loaded down with gift bags. One look at his roaming gaze and the fracture in his

cool demeanor told me he was nervous. He kissed my cheek, squeezing me tightly before he released me to turn, walking farther in to face our daughter.

"Johnny," I said, motioning to Betta. "This is Elizabetta." I twisted a hand when she cringed, hurrying to amend, "Who only likes being called Betta."

He nodded, looking away from me, that gaze lingering like he needed a little support before he approached her. "My mama," he told her, "was also Elizabetta. I think your mother named you for her." When our daughter frowned, glancing at me for clarification, Johnny hurried to continue. "And for her mama as well, Roseline." He leaned closer, taking a box from one of the bags and handing me the others. His smile was nervous but sure when he offered her the small box. "This is for you. I know you have one already, but maybe you can add this..."

Betta was a nine-year-old girl. She liked dragons, unicorns, and books that made her laugh. But she also loved dresses, flowers, and things that made her feel pretty. The patchwork baby doll dress she wore today, one of four outfits she'd tried on, was proof enough of that. Johnny giving her this small, dainty box, a box that held a new locket big enough for three pictures, was perfect. It was platinum, and the pendant was a large oval that opened into three sections. On the surface was intricate filigree and elegant scrollwork that wrapped around a large "C."

"You've got space enough for the pictures of your mama and your *nonna* Ava, and if you want, I've put my mama, your *nonna* Theresa Elizabetta in there too. She was beautiful and very kind. Like your mama... like you too, *piccolo bellezza*."

Betta looked up at him, her eyebrows bunching together at the endearment. I froze, remembering why it stood out to her. I tensed, ready to intercede, but our daughter looked back down at the locket, fingering the picture. "My uncle..." She paused, seeming to silently correct herself before she continued. "Father Patrick used to call me that. 'Little beauty,' he said it meant."

"It does," Johnny answered, kneeling beside her, not touching her, not doing anything but getting to her level, his gaze devouring her face like he'd never seen anything more beautiful in his life. "But if you don't want me to call you that, I won't."

She looked at him, their faces close together. From this angle, the similarities were striking. The same nose. Same wide, full mouth. The same cheekbones. It was remarkable.

"Are you really my father?" she asked Johnny, moving her eyes up and down, gaze taking in his features as quickly as he had done.

"'Fraid you got my mouth, little one. My nose too. We get it from my papa. It's the Carelli side."

Betta nodded, looking back down at the locket, tracing the 'C' with her fingertip as Johnny glanced at me, his expression a little lost. All I could do was offer him a smile, hoping that was encouragement enough to keep him talking to her.

"Why did you stay away so long?" she asked, not looking at him, as though she didn't want to see him cringe, as though she was scared there was a lie he had prepared and she didn't want to see what that would look like.

But Johnny had promised me a new start. He'd promised me the dream, and he wanted it to begin for us right now. He covered Betta's hand with his own, making her look up at him. My girl focused on his face, her expression surprised, her mouth open. She didn't seem ready for him to tell her the truth, and it showed.

"There are a lot of bad people in this world, *la mia bellissima bambina*. And those people want to hurt me and my family. Your mama and...Father Patrick, they wanted to keep you away from those people. They'd do anything to protect you because that's what family does. Family is loyal. Family is forever. And if that means breaking the hearts of the people you love most, then sometimes, that's what you have to do." Johnny touched her face, his thumb moving along her cheekbone, and I couldn't stop the tears that clouded my vision as he watched her. He was amazed. He was awed, and I knew he always would be when he stared at her. "Your mama did the right thing. She did her best."

Our daughter's nod came slowly but surely, and after Johnny's words seem to resonate, a smile moved across her face, as though she was satisfied and happy for the answer she'd always wanted. "Will you help me with this?" she asked him, slipping off the old locket and passing it over to him.

"*Si,*" he told her, his smile wide as he hurried to fit the old pictures into the new charm. "Lift your hair."

She turned, and Johnny draped the necklace in front of her, fiddling with the clasp as Betta grinned up at me. "So," she started, her smile brightening. "What should I call you?"

He glanced at me, then back down at the clasp, focusing on the job he was doing. "You can call me Papa. I would like that, but only if you want to. If you don't, you can call me Johnny."

"Papa," Betta said, trying out the word, rolling the syllables around in her mouth. Then, without any warning at all, she looked back up at me, hands on her hips. "I think you two should get married."

"I agree," Johnny said, not missing a beat. He smiled, brushing her hair down flat after the necklace was secure.

"I also think you should have another baby."

"Betta!" I exclaimed, but I was ignored as she turned to Johnny.

"Maybe a little brother? In a year or so. Can you do that?"

My eyes bulged and Johnny laughed, patting her shoulder as she led him to the table.

"I'd like that. Or," he said, grabbing me around the waist, "maybe a brother *and* a sister." Betta made a face, and Johnny winked at her. "You'll get to boss them around."

She leaned back against her chair, arms folded, like this had become a negotiation and she needed a second to consider the offer. Johnny ushered me to my chair, standing behind me as Betta watched us, finally extending her hand to him.

"Okay," she said, her smile wide when he sat down and shook her hand. "But I'm *not* changing diapers, and my allowance will be steep."

"That can be arranged, little one," he told her, leaning over to kiss our daughter on the top of her head.

Epilogue
Johnny

My father would have laughed at me. But since the old man wasn't here to do it, my sister was filling in.

"I've never seen a grown man cry at his own wedding."

"Fuck you, she's beautiful," I told Cara, ignoring my little sister when her laughter lifted above the crowd.

"Johnny Carelli," her husband said, shaking his head at me like I'd committed some horrible sin that changed his opinion of me. "Sprung like a reformed fuckboy at a titty bar."

"Hey," Cara said, nudging her husband. "Watch your mouth."

"He literally told you to fuck off," Kiel said to his wife, grinning like an idiot.

"Both of you fuck off," I told them, heading in the opposite direction of the two sisters who were congregating near the bar where Cara and Kiel had cornered me.

We'd decked out the Weylin after a full mass at St. Mary's. Sammy, despite everything, all the lies told by Patrick and on his behalf, was still a Catholic. She wanted this done right, and she wanted the world to see. There would be no large wedding party—just Indra standing up for her, Betta as her flower girl, and Smoke as my best man. The mass completed, which Patrick did not perform for obvious reasons—though, he told anyone who'd listen he still wasn't feeling quite recovered from his heart attack—we'd invited our friends, family, and associates to the Weylin.

Surrounding us now was a crowd I hardly recognized. The Garcias had made an enthusiastic appearance, Mrs. Garcia telling Sammy she knew that night at dinner that it wouldn't be long before we married. We didn't bother explaining about the flower girl, and by the end of the night, I had a signed contract in my hand and a new investor in Mr. Garcia. One step closer to my family being out of *the* family.

"Johnny." I heard, and I twisted around to see my cousin Smoke leaning against the wall. His attention was on a table to the left and a few of her volunteers Sammy had introduced me to earlier in the day. They were young and pretty and completely uninterested in anything but a good time, just how a guy like Smoke seemed to like them. "I wanted to tell you," he started, grinning at the tallest of the girls when she looked him over. "Dante got word that Liam is in Ireland."

"That right?" I turned away from the crowd, facing my cousin, not caring about anything at that moment but what he knew about that asshole and the threat he might pose to my wife and daughter.

"I knew you were busy, so I took care of it."

"And how did you do that?" I asked him, not convinced he had the clout to take care of much when it came to someone like Liam. He might be a punk, but Shane was still part of the McKinney *family*. They cared what happened to theirs.

"I had words with Ian." Smoke finished his drink, looking down to the bottom like he couldn't believe he'd polished it off.

"Ian...McKinney?"

"Si," he said, setting the glass on the table to his left.

"Ian McKinney, who..."

"You always look surprised when I do shit. Why is that, cousin? You think I'm stupid?" He was joking, grinning at me like he expected me to say yes, and laughed when I didn't.

"I think I'm more serious than ever about you taking over for me."

Smoke moved his jaw, his head working in one long nod. "That right?" The sound of laughter from the table caught his attention, and my cousin shifted his gaze, his head still facing me before he pushed off the wall, tucking one hand into his pocket. "Let me think about it," he said, heading toward the table.

"You feel like dancing?" I asked him, head shaking when he gave me a "man, please" look.

"I don't dance." Then he stopped by the table, leaning down to whisper something in the tall girl's ear, and the pair of them disappeared into the crowd, in the opposite direction of the dance floor.

My gaze caught in the middle of the room, to my little girl twirling in her pale green tutu dress, with the ribbons in her hair as she moved in time with the music. She was beautiful. Her long, dark hair was curled, hitting her waist as she held her little cousin, Keleu.

Kit and Kane were nestled off to the side, watching and talking to their friends Dale and Gin, who was heavily pregnant with her first child. They could all use this trip to my wedding as a business write-off if they were so inclined since my production company was now funding their new cable shows. Little by little, my legitimate companies were taking over. If I could settle them all, squeeze myself out of the businesses that had made my father rich, then I wouldn't have to worry about my family, my blood family, being in danger.

I made my way to the dance floor as Kiel picked up the baby from Betta. "Dance with your old man?" I asked her, holding out my hand.

She laughed when I twirled her, then hopped onto the tops of my feet, letting me lead her. "Aren't you supposed to be smooching my mama?"

"That comes later," I told her, barking out a laugh when Betta wrinkled her nose.

"Where is she?" The girl swiveled her head, frowning when she couldn't spot Sammy in the crowd.

I picked her up, letting her see above the crowd. "There," I said, lifting my chin toward the bridal table. At the end, huddled in a corner, sat my wife, Sammy, and Father Patrick.

"Wow," Betta said. She nodded, looking down at me when I turned, exaggerating our movements to follow the rhythm. "Did you do that?"

"I did nothing," I said, twirling us in the opposite direction.

My daughter grinned, wrapping her arms around my neck. "I think you did, and it's good."

"Think so, little one?" I asked. Didn't think I'd ever get tired of how good it felt when she hugged me.

"I think it's the best thing you could have done for her, Papa."

"Nah, *picolinna*," I told her, kissing her cheek. "You're the best thing for both of us."

The world was watching, and we didn't care. Judgments and opinions and a bunch of thoughts that had nothing to do us washed over us, and they still didn't touch us.

Nothing would.

"This was a great day," Sammy said, head against my chest, her fingers curled in my hand. "Thank you, Johnny."

"Every day is a great day with you, *amore mia*."

The music was slow, and the crowd was thinning. Kane held his woman two feet from me, shooting me a nod just before he led his wife and two sleeping daughters away from the venue. I didn't know what had become of my cousins, likely drunk or passed out somewhere, probably sleeping between one or more of Sammy's volunteers, but Antonia had skipped the reception altogether, and Dario still wasn't a fan of large crowds. I had a feeling it would take a while for him to shake off Rikers.

The Seattle contingent was gone; Dale and Gin congratulating us and leaving for their hotel, and my sister and brother-in-law taking their cranky baby home for the night.

Now it was just me and my wife and a few lingering friends who still didn't quite believe that Johnny Carelli had given up the single life.

But I had. Gladly. Willingly.

Sammy melted against me, and it took all my effort not to drag her off of the dance floor and find an empty room in this place. I wanted her—now. Wanted more than anything to get busy working on the sibling request Betta had made. But one glance around the room, spotting Father Patrick sitting next to my daughter, doused any of those sparking inclinations.

He sat directly across from us, glaring whenever Betta didn't hold his attention, but I didn't care. Let the old man have his anger. He could hate me all he wanted. I had my wife. I had my child. And Sammy was starting to forgive him.

"Talk to him," I'd prompted, reminding her two days ago that he was old and wouldn't be around much longer. "If you don't say your piece now, you'll always regret it."

A small olive branch had come with an invitation to our wedding, something I was convinced he'd tried to object to. He didn't, and Sammy spent a half hour of the reception letting the old man tell her how sorry he was and how much he missed her and Betta.

It would take a long time for her to forgive, even longer to forget.

But for now, the only thing on my mind was my wife and the life we were moving toward. She stretched her arms around my neck and smiled at me, that same glorious smile that had mesmerized me as a boy. It had always driven me over the edge like it did now, and I moved in closer, kissing her, needing a taste, never being full of her.

"*Bella*," I whispered through a sigh. "I'll never get tired of the way you taste."

"Good," she said, biting her lip, the small gesture reminding me of that first day in the library, years ago.

"You know, you told me once you were going to burn in hell because of me." She looked up, moving her head back as though only just recalling the memory.

Sammy's surprise softened into a smile, her features relaxing as she ran her fingertips over my face. "I'd burn for you. A hundred times, I'd burn for you, my love."

"It doesn't matter where we spend eternity, *bella*." I kissed her, knowing right then nothing or no one would ever make me feel this good or this free. "A lifetime with you is all the heaven I need."

The End

Acknowledgements

Thank you to Chelle for letting me play in this universe and for always fussing at me when I need it the most. No one believes in my writing more than you do. I don't think you'll ever *really* know how much that means to me. Thank you, a million times. I love you!

Thanks to my girls, Chelsey, Trin, Faith, and Grace, to the Moon Baby for your love and patience, and to Chris, who is better than any book boyfriend. Twenty-seven books later and they still love me. I'm a lucky lady.

As always, thank you to my sweet, encouraging readers, my Sweet Team, my Saints & Sinners and my ride-or-dies, my Corporate Hell sisters—Barbara Blakes, Marie Anderson-Simmons, Kalpana Singh, Sarah Cooper, and Sherry Jackson. I'm crossing my fingers we make it to the other side. I love you all!

Eden Butler

About Eden Butler

Eden Butler is an editor and writer of Romance, SciFi and Fantasy novels and the nine-time great-granddaughter of an honest-to-God English pirate. This could explain her affinity for rule breaking and rum.

When she's not writing, or wondering about her *possibly* Jack Sparrowesque ancestor, Eden impatiently awaits her Hogwarts letter, writes, reads and spends too much time watching New Orleans Saints football, and dreaming up plots that will likely keep her on deadline until her hair is white and her teeth are missing.

Currently, she is imprisoned under teenage rule alongside her husband in Southeastern Louisiana. Please send help.

WEBSITE – edenbutler.com

READER GROUP – https://bit.ly/2kzMnsf

Subscribe to Eden's newsletter http://eepurl. com/VXQXD for giveaways, sneak peeks and various goodies that might just give you a chuckle.

About Chelle Bliss

Chelle Bliss is the *Wall Street Journal* and *USA Today* bestselling author of Men of Inked: Southside Series, Misadventures of a City Girl, the Men of Inked, and ALFA Investigations series.

She hails from the Midwest, but currently lives near the beach even though she hates sand. She's a full-time writer, time-waster extraordinaire, social media addict, coffee fiend, and ex history teacher.

She loves spending time with her two cats, alpha boyfriend, and chatting with readers. To learn more about Chelle, please visit menofinked.com or chellebliss.com.

JOIN MY NEWSLETTER
➜ https://www.menofinked.com/news-bm/
Text Notifications (US only)
➜ Text **ALPHAS** to **24587**

WHERE TO FOLLOW CHELLE:
➜ WEBSITE
menofinked.com
➜ TWITTER
twitter.com/ChelleBliss1

➔ FACEBOOK
facebook.com/authorchellebliss1
➔ INSTAGRAM
instagram.com/authorchellebliss/

Want to drop me a line?
➔ authorchellebliss@gmail.com
➔ www.chellebliss.com

TO SIGN UP for my VIP newsletter, featuring exclusive eBooks, special deals, and giveaways!
https://www.menofinked.com/news-bm/
or
text GALLOS to 24587
to sign up for VIP text news